Pirate's Counsel

Book 1 in the Hunter Series

Kimberly Grey

Hard Shell Word Factory

ISBN: 0-7599-0455-3
Trade Paperback
Published February 2005

ISBN: 1-58200-535-4
Published January 1999

Hard Shell Word Factory
PO Box 161
Amherst Jct. WI 54407
books@hardshell.com
www.hardshell.com

All characters in this book have no existence outside the imagination of the author, and have no relation whatever to anyone bearing the same name or names. These characters are not even distantly inspired by any individual known or unknown to the author, and all incidents are pure invention.

Chapter 1

IT WAS A mob scene. A circus.

Christine Dunn heaved a sigh and her briefcase through the crowd of men and women, mostly reporters, who were jamming the halls of the Los Angeles County Courthouse. They were all looking for a photograph, a quote or an interview with anyone involved in the highly sensationalized case going on behind the closed doors she could barely see over the sea of heads, microphones and hats.

Struggling to maneuver through the undulating waves of bodies and muttering under her breath about the freedom of the press, she swung around a pillar in an attempt to find a way to the front door of the building and wondered. Was it the public driving the media frenzy around her or was it just the networks looking for higher ratings?

She suppressed a sigh and squeezed between two arguing reporters. It really didn't matter. Whatever the reason, the hype and chaos it caused was making it hard to get her job done.

On any normal day, her trip to the courthouse would have taken no more than ten minutes, but she'd been locked in the building for over an hour. During that time she'd been accosted at least four times by eager news hounds looking for an inside tip, a new source of information, or some tasty tidbit about the latest melodrama to capture the nation.

It was Hollywood all over again, but this time it wasn't murder. It was polygamy.

A well-known and adored male star had married one of the country's favorite female vocalists, apparently forgetting in the interim to tell the singer he was wed already. And, there was the additional complication of a paternity suit by a third woman who claimed he'd taken her through one of the wedding chapels in Las Vegas a year before.

All three would-be wives claimed to be victims, but as Christine paused to set her overloaded briefcase down to adjust the additional armload of papers and folders she was carrying, she didn't think any one of the trio causing the media explosion were as helpless or defenseless as her latest client.

Patty Zaworski was twenty-seven, ninety pounds wringing wet, the mother of two and the wife to a man who was three times her size and who got rid of his frustrations by beating her up. Patty had endured the abuse for years. But when, in a fit of rage, Bill Zaworski had thrown a chair across the room and put their youngest child in the hospital, Patty had finally found the strength to seek escape. Christine's mouth set in a determined line. She was going to make sure Patty's getaway was good.

Lifting a hand to brush wisps of hair that were blonde and knotted into a French braid from her face, Christine paused for a moment to focus on the crowd pressing in around her.

She recognized several other attorneys amongst the people. They, like her, were trying to get business conducted in other parts of the courthouse, but first they had to wade through the crush of humanity waiting for a story. Yet not all the lawyers present were trying to avoid the media. Those who were among the more well known in the city willingly stopped on request to preen for a television crew and offer an opinion.

She smiled as one eagle-eyed reporter swooped through the constantly shifting throng to corral one such attorney before the glass eye of a camera, but forced to lean to the right as the crowd shifted to allow others to weave through, she was grateful to be one of the many who could walk in and out of the building without being recognized.

She wasn't well known. None of the reporters circling through the hall would purposely track her down due to name recognition. And she was glad.

Hers was a small practice. A one-person office that was finally beginning to grow, and she liked the independence and challenge of it—even if, at times, the bills were hard to handle. Abruptly remembering those bills, she shifted the folders in her arms once again, blew out a determined breath and reached blindly down to grab her briefcase.

The weight of it seemed to have increased considerably since she'd set it down. An impossibility, she nevertheless found herself wishing she could afford to hire a legal clerk. It would save her from running all of her own errands, but it was a luxury she still couldn't afford.

Glancing wistfully at one of the more famous local legal counselors being interviewed, she longed to have just one of his huge staff. A paralegal would allow her to spend more time practicing law instead of shuffling paper, but dreams for what could be were quickly forgotten when she spotted an opening in the crowd.

Dodging toward sunlight, she dashed through the door and onto the sidewalk that, lit by the brilliant morning glare, led her toward the building that housed her office just a few blocks away.

Finding space so close to the county seat had been a miracle, and finding someone to share the cost of the rent had been an additional blessing— and a curse.

Stumbling over hard concrete, wishing she'd worn flats instead of fashionable white pumps that looked better than they felt on her feet, she frowned as she thought of the man who occupied the office with her. A private investigator, she'd used his services on occasion, but she wasn't entirely happy with their partnership. And she was reminded of why when she opened the door painted with both her and his names and came face-to-face with her co-tenant.

"Good morning, beautiful."

The greeting was not unusual. Not coming from him, and Christine managed to arch a cool eyebrow at David Maverick in response. But it wasn't easy. Not when he was watching her.

Over six foot, lean but well-muscled, and dark with a thick mass of hair that was brown enough to nearly pass for black, she didn't think the pulse of many women would remain steady under his intense gaze. Even the scar that marred his right eyebrow and left a thin white line across his forehead did nothing to detract from his manly charms. The mark gave him character rather than a handicap, and the black patch he wore to cover the brown eye he'd lost was intriguing more than repulsing. There in lay the problem.

She didn't want to be interested in him or in any other man. She was a career woman. She was her own master, and no man would ever dictate her life. Not ever again. Yet he tempted just by his presence, but she wasn't about to rise to the bait.

Stopping to cock her head, she studied him warily. "Fishing for a return compliment?"

"If only I could be so lucky."

His smile put slashes in his cheeks and sent delicious chills down her spine, but she didn't let him see the effect.

Instead she hid the shiver and stepped forward to get around him. Her office would offer sanctuary from his influence—which proved to be unexpectedly formidable when she got a whiff of his aftershave. Forcing herself to ignore it and him, she managed a quick quip. "Sorry. Too busy for an affair. Try me next week."

He grinned and was forced to move aside to let her by because the suite they occupied together didn't offer a lot of standing room.

The “reception area” was less than moderately sized and filled to capacity by some chairs, a coffee table and two desks. The desks belonged to their secretaries, neither of who were in the office for the day yet, but that wasn’t unusual.

Candy and Mandy set their own schedules. Identical twins who were whizzes on the computer, demon typists when it came to speed and accuracy in knocking out legal briefs, they both worked part time, and they both worked for she *and* David.

It was an odd working arrangement that, as mothers, allowed the two women to get to the office, individually or jointly, no later than ten each morning. The only condition in the routine required at least one of the twins to be in the office during business hours to cover the phones and to complete any typing that needed to get done.

Somehow, if at times confusing when it came to remembering what secretary would be in when, the situation always seemed to work for everyone, and Christine liked to think that giving her employees flex hours made her a modern day boss.

She slipped into the room off to the right. David’s office was to the left and beyond the small file room standing in between. She heaved a sigh of profound relief when she reached her desk and dropped the pile of folders she’d been carrying.

“Working late last night?” David asked from the doorway as she added her small, shoulder strap purse to the load.

“New clients passed on from a friend,” she admitted and knew he understood her appreciation of the referrals. For, if acquaintances from law school were kind enough to toss her the smaller fish they didn’t want to fry in their large, cushy law firms, those he used to work with in the Los Angeles Police Department did the same for him and sent new clients his way whenever they could.

Nodding his approval, David wandered in to look down at the stack of papers, and watching him, she tucked her tongue in her cheek to keep from giving into the curiosity that hit her about him now and again.

She knew he was an ex-cop, guessed he’d left because of the loss of his eye and assumed he was getting a disability pension that helped over the rough spots. But she never asked. Manners. And distance. She liked to keep boundaries between them. Too much personal knowledge could ruin the civility of their working relationship.

“This ought to keep the twins busy,” he said, putting out a tanned hand to run a thumb over the edges of the folders.

“Me, too,” she sighed, lifting the briefcase onto the desk as well to lay it on its side in preparation of flipping it open. "And maybe you."

The smile was back, flashing in a face as tan as his hand and as the column of throat that lay exposed with the first two buttons of his white shirt open.

She nearly sighed disapproval. David seldom wore a tie. His idea of proper business attire was more casual than her own. Yet it was difficult to find fault with his choice of apparel when he looked as good in a sports jacket as some men did in a tux.

"Anything interesting?" he asked.

"They're not all divorces, if that's what you mean," she assured him with understanding. She, too, liked a little variety in her work. "One missing person, one possible security consult from a burglary and a personal injury investigation. Car accident."

"Have I told you today that you're beautiful?" he asked, shoving his hands in his pants pockets as she popped the latches on the briefcase.

Avoiding the golden brown eye she always felt missed little and sometimes saw too much, she shoved the lid of the case up. "Flattery will get you..." Abruptly, she stuttered, forgetting what she was going to say. Because, reaching into the attaché for the expected, she found the unexpected instead. *A lot* of the unexpected.

"Get me what?" he prompted when she didn't finish her sentence, but she didn't hear him.

Stunned, staring, struggling to understand what lay before her, she forgot he was even in the room with her until he leaned across the desk to look at what she was and whistled.

"Stop at the bank on the way to work, Chris?"

She sputtered, trying to get her tongue to work, but no words would form in her mouth. Speaking was simply impossible. Thinking was, too, when confronted with more money than she'd ever seen in her life—and it was all sitting inside her briefcase. "This isn't mine!" she finally managed to protest, willing her heart out of her throat.

"Looks like yours," he disagreed calmly, cocking his head to study the small suitcase from a different angle.

"But it's not!" she denied. "I packed mine this morning, and it wasn't loaded with ... with ..." Suddenly the air locked in her lungs, and he had to come to her rescue.

Moving around the desk to take her by the shoulders, he eased her down into her chair. "Deep breaths."

She did as he suggested. Breathed. But she couldn't pull her eyes away from the cash—or let go of him. Grabbing his hand when he would have straightened and stepped back, she squeezed hard. "David, this isn't mine."

"Then where'd you get it?"

"I..." But she couldn't answer because she didn't know. Yet she tried to reason. And remember. Where had she been, what had she done since leaving home two hours earlier? And when had she last looked inside the case? "The clerk's office!" she blurted. "I opened it at the courthouse. There wasn't any money in it then. I have witnesses!"

His lips twitched, and his fingers engulfed hers. "No one's accusing you of anything, counselor."

"Of course not," she agreed primly and snatched her hand from the warm reassurance of his, but she was unable to relax back into the chair. The edge was preferable. So she could run if she had to. Straight back to the courthouse from where the alien bag had come. Still, if her pulse continued to hammer madly, her brain was beginning to work again. "I stopped on the way out of the building, and I set the case down." She shook her head. "The place was a madhouse."

"The Hollywood Harem case," he said more than asked.

"Yes, and the hallways were jammed. Reporters all over. It was like crawling through a maze trying to get out."

"And?"

She frowned, trying to recall exactly what she'd done and everything and seen. "I was nearly to the front door, but the folders I was carrying were slipping."

"You said you put the bag down. Where?" he asked.

"Right beside me," she assured him.

"But you didn't keep an eye on it?"

"No, I was looking around."

He leaned back against the desk and crossed his arms over his chest. "For how long?"

She bit her lip. "A minute or two maybe."

"And when you picked it up again?"

"I remember it felt heavier, but I didn't think much about it. I just assumed it was my imagination."

"When you picked it up, did you look at it? Did you notice if there were other cases like it sitting nearby that somebody else might have put down?"

"No, I just reached and grabbed." She shrugged helplessly. "It wasn't as if I'd put it out of sight."

"Did you see anyone else carrying an attaché like yours?"

Scowling, she chewed at her lower lip. "There were a lot of other attorneys there. Most had some sort of briefcase, but I didn't pay any particular attention to what type." She narrowed her eyes, reviewing the scene in her mind. "But they weren't the only ones with some type of bag. The media crews had their usual carry alls scattered around."

"What about people?" he pressed. "Did you notice anyone in particular near you?"

"Everybody was near everybody!" she objected and leaned forward to look more closely at the money. All wrapped up in fat packs and placed in not quite tidy rows, the well-worn bills filled the briefcase to capacity. She swallowed. Most of the greenbacks were hundred dollar bills. Considering how many were stuffed inside, she guessed the amount she'd carried out of the courthouse numbered in the thousands. "But I didn't think anyone was close enough to slip me this!"

"They'll probably be a lot closer soon," he assured her, and the certainty in his voice had her jerking back to look up at him again.

"What do you mean?"

"Was your name in your briefcase?"

"Of course. It's on the papers..." Realization had her thoughts log jamming and fear igniting.

"If I lost that much money and knew who had it," he said quietly. "I think I'd probably come after it."

Her heart dropped into her stomach. "But..."

The front door crashed open, and she bolted to her feet, slamming the briefcase shut and clenching her hands around the handle. His reaction was more subtle.

Without a word, he reached out to squeeze her shoulder. His grip was steadying. Encouraging. But he didn't linger. He slipped away, leaving her cold and alone while he silently took up a position out of sight behind a filing cabinet.

Christine wanted to stop him, to speak, to ask him what she should say or do when confronted, but she couldn't. There was no time. Someone was approaching, growing closer. She could hear whoever it was breathing. Harshly. As if they'd been running. After her?

She didn't know. She was just grateful she wasn't by herself. David was with her. His nearness gave her confidence. He would protect her if need be. With the gun he was licensed to carry if he had to. Yet, suddenly, he wasn't the only man in the room.

A stranger came to fill the doorway. Big, barrel chested, his weight was at least two hundred fifty pounds. And he wasn't happy. Beneath a ragged crewcut, his face was wide and grim, and the finger he raised to point her way was bitterly accusing. "You're her!"

Trapped but not ready to be declared defenseless, adrenaline brought strength on a wave of anger, and she squared her shoulders to acknowledge the allegation. "I'm Christine Dunn."

A growl was his response. A growl and an advance straight towards her.

It was all she could do not to back up watching him come. The urge to flee was strong, especially when trapped by his menacing glare, but she stood her ground and waited for his heavy footsteps to bring him to the other side of her desk. Tilting her chin up in unconscious challenge, she glared back. "Can I help you?"

"Yeah, you can get out of my life," the man snarled.

She blinked, surprised by the demand that had nothing to do with the money in her briefcase.

"And you can stay away from my wife," he hissed.

Recognition came with a flash of insight and from memory of snap shots because the man before her didn't believe in answering a summons and appearing in court. Distaste filled her mouth. "Bill Zaworski."

"That's me," he declared and put two thick fists down to lean on them and closer to her. "And you have no business talking to my wife."

"Your wife hired me," Christine denied coolly, no longer intimidated, only determined. "And she has rights."

"I say what she's got!"

The bellow didn't even make Christine flinch. She'd stopped running from bullies long ago. She put her knuckles on top of the desk, too. "What she has is a restraining order against you, and if you go anywhere near her or the children, you'll be placed under arrest."

His response was unexpected. And quick. He gave her no warning and absolutely no time to duck. Not before the back of his hand connected with her cheek.

The blow had lights exploding in her head. The force of it sent her spinning backwards.

Miraculously she hit the chair. It caught and saved her from a collision with the floor, but nothing could stop the panic. Not when her mind was working but her body wasn't. In limbo between conscious thought and unconscious oblivion, she couldn't see, couldn't make her arms or legs respond to her brain's frantic commands. But she could hear.

Nearby a savage growl ripped the air. It was rapidly followed by a roar, a crash and the sickening sound of flesh meeting flesh. Yet she remained limp, unable to command the dead weight of her limbs or control the fear that rocketed through her.

She was caught, trapped within an unrelenting blackness that threatened to consume and carry her into an unnatural sleep. Helpless she had no idea what was happening. Listening to the grunts of battle, she could only guess, and that wasn't good enough.

Fighting to sit up, she tried to break free of the force trying to pull her down. Her efforts made her blink—just as sudden silence descended.

Terror grabbed her by the throat. The sounds of fighting echoed no more. The room was quiet. Still. No one moved. No one spoke, but someone had to be inside it with her. Somebody had won the battle. Was it friend or foe?

Desperate, she clawed her way out of the fog and back into the light and gasped when the office swam into blurred images that included a pair of legs. Yet relief died quickly. If it was David stretched out on the floor in front of her desk....

"Are you all right?

She nearly screamed when a hard hand clutched her shoulder. Whirling, she instinctively raised her arms in self-defense, but she had no need for alarm. It wasn't an enemy she faced. It was David. She collapsed back into the chair. "I don't know."

And she didn't. Her mind was still scrambling to process and separate information. She felt numb, disoriented, but coherent thought was returning—along with waves of pain.

An angry throb was starting to pound in her face. It centered on the cheekbone a meaty fist had collided with, but when she lifted a hand to check for damage, David stopped her.

Catching and squeezing her fingers in his with a gentleness that made her toes curl and her pulse skip, he grimaced. "I'm sorry. I should have seen that coming."

Unexpectedly more conscious of the heat of his flesh against hers than of the growing ache in her head, she wanted to deny him the blame, but he didn't give her the chance. He turned away and left her. Yet he didn't go far, and he wasn't gone long. In seconds he returned with a towel from the small bathroom concealed behind a side door and with some ice from the small refrigerator sitting in the office corner.

"Here," he murmured, bending close. "Try this."

Guiding his hand and the cold pack to her cheek, she winced at the initial contact but didn't back away from the frigid cloth. It offered relief from the hurt that was both insistent and building in intensity and, somehow, his touch soothed, too.

Closing her eyes as the throb began to recede, she relaxed into the cushions of the chair and concentrated on the feel of his hand under hers as he held the compress in place. It was larger than hers, stronger, but the skin covering it was amazingly soft. And warm.

The deep rumble of his voice penetrated the cocoon of shock she was drifting into, and she realized he must have used his free hand to grab the phone.

"The police are coming," he told her quietly as the receiver bumped back into its cradle, and confronted with the harsh consequences of reality, she tried to collect scattered thoughts and emotions.

"Assault. That should keep him away from Patty for awhile."

"Always thinking of your client."

She opened her eyes again to look up at him. "She needs me."

"To stop him," David agreed and nodded to the unconscious figure sprawled on the carpet. "I think you've done that, and I think the judge is going to make sure she gets custody of her kids—away from him."

"Good," Christine declared, ignoring the jabs of pain that came with talking. "She doesn't need him. She doesn't need a man to make a life."

David's gaze narrowed, but she didn't see. Not while she was glaring at Bill Zaworski's still form. And if David was about to speak, she didn't have a chance to hear what he was about to say. Not when Mandy and Candy suddenly appeared in the doorway.

Both blonde, both blue eyed, age had seen the twins outgrow the need to dress alike, but they still moved as a unit.

Glancing from the man sprawled on the carpet to their employers, they asked in unison, "Did we miss something?"

CHRISTINE EASED herself down into her desk chair. It looked incredibly comfortable. It felt it, too, when she sank into its worn cushions with an audible groan.

The police station was behind her. She'd left it a short time before after giving her statement, after having her photograph taken to document the evidence of assault and after seeing Bill Zaworski hauled away.

She blew out a breath. David's call had brought two squads to the office. One had taken Bill Zaworski to a holding cell. The other had carried she and David to the local division where all the paperwork could be processed to insure Zaworski would be booked and remained locked up until he could be arraigned.

Slowly putting her head back to rest against the chair, she nearly groaned again. It'd taken nearly two hours to get the job done. Two hours of silent agony.

Inside her skull the echoes of pain were still ricocheting, bouncing from one side of her brain to the other like a ping pong ball, but she could expect no less. Not considering Bill Zaworski's grand slam to her cheek bone.

She closed her eyes. Thankfully David had stayed with her the entire time at the station. His presence and his familiarity with both the people and the procedure had made the whole ordeal easier and quicker.

A frown curved her mouth. It was odd, but he hadn't tried to tell her what to say during the interview with the detective. Not once had he made any attempt to take over the statement process. His male ego hadn't forced him to take charge. Instead he'd waited for her to speak and explain before joining in the conversation to corroborate her story and add further detail.

His restraint surprised her. He did.

Her journey to the police station certainly would have been more difficult without him. His assistance and support as well as his credibility, due to his background as a uniformed officer, had saved her from a potentially endless round of questions and delays. That and the fact that everyone liked him. Most of the officers at the division had known and greeted him with genuine warmth and respect. He was their peer still even out of uniform.

Letting herself relax into the high backed chair, she sighed relief as the weight of her pounding head was absorbed by the padded leather. The right side of her face was hot. The numbing effect of the discarded ice used earlier had long ago worn off.

Biting her lip, she was tempted to go get more, but it required too much effort. It was much easier to stay where she was and to wonder. Why did being a lawyer have such appeal? Surely there were easier ways to right the proverbial wrongs of the world other than by standing on the front line of defense.

"You okay?"

"It depends on your perspective," she murmured, not surprised by

David's question but not moving a fraction either. He'd come back with her from the station, stopping to speak to Candy and Mandy while she'd gone on to her office to collapse in private. "If you're outside my head, life's not so bad."

"Did you take those aspirin?"

She almost nodded but stopped herself in time and, listening to without watching him, decided his voice was as soothing on the ears as he was on the eyes. A smile curved her lips. Her hero.

"Something funny?"

She reluctantly opened her eyes to look up at him as he stood studying her from the opposite side of the desk. "I was just thinking that you've now been elevated from co-tenant and PI to hero."

He grimaced. "A hero wouldn't have let you get hit in the first place."

"He wouldn't have hit me at all if I hadn't put my chin out for him to swing at."

David's teeth flashed in a quick grin. "Such a pretty chin, too." He leaned over to touch the piece of anatomy in question and turned her head to admire what, she imagined, was a growing bruise. He shook his head. "And a pretty gutsy move when you consider our friend was twice your size."

"He's a bully, and I don't like bullies," she declared, but the warmth spreading from his skin to hers was distracting. And unnerving. He seemed so strong while she felt so weak. Yet she wasn't afraid. Not in his presence, and that didn't make sense. Or, then again, maybe it did. After all, he'd rescued her. Saved her. She was grateful—and embarrassed. She'd been blind sided and knocked on her derriere right in front of him. It was preferable to take her humiliations in private.

"I never cared for bullies much myself." His hand dropped away, and he straightened once more to cock his head at her. "Why don't you call it a day?"

"I can't," she objected, avoiding his observant gaze and ignoring the tingling sensation left from his touch by reluctantly sitting forward to gesture to her desk and the stack of folders. "I've got..."

But she suddenly realized what she didn't have.

Lurching to her feet, panic grabbed her by the throat. "My briefcase! The money!"

"Here," David said, bending to pick it up from the floor. "I moved it."

Relief had her collapsing back into her seat and lifting a hand to massage her throbbing temple. "How could I have forgotten? I should have told the police about it. I should have taken it with me when we went to the station. I'll have to call them back."

"Why?" he asked as she reached for the phone.

"Why?" she echoed in disbelief, but he was serious. His expression was sober, nearly grim, but she was far from convinced. "Because it's not mine. Because there must be hundreds of thousands of dollars in that case that belongs to someone else."

"Yes," he agreed. "Someone who doesn't mind carrying a small fortune into a courthouse instead of a bank. Unusual, don't you think?"

"I..."

"Why do you suppose somebody would take that kind of money to a court?"

The first answer that popped into her mind wasn't one she liked. "A bribe?"

He shrugged and placed the case on the desk between them. "Or what about an exchange?"

She frowned. "An exchange?"

"You could have left the building with a load of cocaine just as easily as money."

Air hissed through her lips in a startled gasp. "A drug deal? In a courthouse?"

"It's a public place. People coming and going all of the time, and you said it yourself. It was a madhouse this morning," he told her. "Who would notice if two people set down cases next to each other and walked off with the wrong one? Nobody saw you grab and leave with what wasn't yours, did they?"

"No," she agreed. "Except maybe the person..."

"Who must have mistaken you for the guy he, or she, was supposed to meet and swap luggage with."

The pounding in her head suddenly increased in rhythm. And, overwhelmed with possibilities and scenarios—all of them illegal, immoral and involving a criminal element she wasn't, at least for the moment, prepared to deal with—she glared at him. "And you don't think I need the police?"

"No, what you need is protection."

"Protection?"

"Somebody's going to want our briefcase back," he said, patting the attaché affectionately.

Frowning, she immediately wanted to object to the "our." Her problem wasn't his. But for argument's sake, and for that of her sanity, she let it pass to listen. He'd helped her out during the morning's chaos. Considering she had the rest of the day to get through, she was open to opinions. "What are you suggesting?"

"I'm going to be your bodyguard."

Chapter 2

DAVID WATCHED Christine's mouth work. She wanted to object to the suggestion, but he wasn't going to let her. Too much was at stake, like catching the bad guys. "Unless, of course, you'd like to be here by yourself when somebody comes to get this."

Her eyes widened on the briefcase. "If the money is being used in some illegal activity, do you really think someone will dare come after it?"

"Wouldn't you if you'd lost that much money?" he asked, pressing his point home and erasing her doubt. "Besides the people we're talking about would probably dare anything. But then, they might not now. The police were here after all."

She frowned, and he could almost see her mind work. It was a good mind. Quick. Sharp. Loaded with knowledge of legal ins and outs, and it was wrapped in a pretty package.

No one would ever call Christine Dunn beautiful. Her hair was long and blonde, if always under restraint as it was at the moment. Twisted into an intricate French braid, the style accented her eyes that were the same clear blue as a summer sky, but her face wasn't extraordinary. The mouth was too wide, the nose a bit too long. And her figure wasn't Hugh Hefner material either. She was too slim. Yet he was sure there were some intriguing bends and curves beneath the carefully cut business suits and jackets she constantly wore.

The consummate professional, never once had he seen her in slacks, but that was okay because he liked her legs. Long, slender, coltish. Her limbs were the kind a man could dream about being wrapped around him while laying in bed—not that he'd ever given into that fantasy. At least not with her, or not that he was willing to admit at any rate.

"How would they know that?" she asked, her hand again rubbing at the ache he was sure was throbbing inside her head. Having been on the wrong side of hard knuckles on a few occasions, he knew how she was feeling, and his fists clenched in anger that she had to endure the pain.

Zaworski never should have touched her, but he'd made the mistake of thinking the man was all mouth and no brawn. He'd been wrong, and Christine had paid the price for his error. The bruise darkening her pale skin nearly made him back off on pushing her about the briefcase. But he couldn't. Even if she was hurting, something juicy was going on in the Los Angeles County Courthouse, and whatever it was wasn't being done by any law-abiding citizens. "Because they're watching."

Her hand froze and her gaze fastened on him in alarm.

"It wouldn't have taken long for them to realize a mistake had been made," he told her quietly. "They would have gone through your case, gotten your name and address and come here as quickly as possible."

"And seen the squads..."

"And Bill Zaworski being escorted outside."

"But how could they be sure..."

"We hadn't turned over the briefcase?" He shrugged. "They didn't see it leave the building."

She shivered and lifted her hands to rub her arms to chase away the chill that, he was sure, had nothing to do with the air conditioning quietly cooling the room.

"Maybe they should see it go," she determined with a decisive nod. "If I give it to the police, whoever the money belongs to can get it back from the cops and leave me alone."

He watched her reach for the phone once more. "Don't you want to know who's running a racket out of the county courthouse?"

She scowled at him, a line forming between blue eyes clouded with conflicting emotions, but he was pretty sure he knew how to get her to start thinking along the same lines he was.

"Never mind," he told her with a wave of his hand when she lifted the receiver and started punching buttons. "I understand. It is safer, easier to let someone else handle it."

"Wait a minute," she said, her gaze narrowing on him and her index finger stopping in mid-jab. "This has nothing to do with being safe or easy. This has to do with what's right."

"Of course," he agreed with as much docility as he could muster, but curiosity was working against her best intentions. Just like he figured it would.

She dropped the receiver back into the cradle. "If not the police," she asked. "What do you have in mind?"

"We set a trap."

"A trap," she repeated, slowly, succinctly, and rose to pace to one side of the room and back again. And he watched her go. In a white suit with pink shell, she looked cool and remote, but he knew she had passion. He'd seen it in court, witnessed it less than an hour before when she'd stood up to a man nearly two hundred pounds heavier than she, and he'd felt it in the natural chemistry that bubbled between them on a regular basis—an event she consistently tried to ignore.

She stopped at the desk once more to stare at the briefcase. "How?"

He hid a smile and stopped himself from reaching out to give her a hug by crossing his arms over his chest. Being mauled wasn't something she'd appreciate, even if the gesture would be meant as an offer of comfort. Ms. Christine Dunn liked to stand on her own. It hadn't taken him more than a few days of knowing her to figure that out, but if she liked keeping a wall between them, it was difficult for him, in this instance, not to break it down.

Shaken and dazed by the short day's events, she looked vulnerable, confused, and the red mark on her cheek reminded him that she was operating under a handicap. Still he couldn't let that stop him. Not when, even out of uniform, the law enforcement instinct remained strong. A crook was out there somewhere needing to be caught, and the only way he was going to be able to do it was with her help. "We wait for contact."

She took a deep breath and eyed him with some degree of doubt. "That will be soon?"

"I'm not sure," he admitted, sitting on the desk's corner. "They'd like to come in right away, but with your not turning the case over to the cops as they might have expected, they have a problem."

"What kind of problem?"

"You. They're trying to figure out why you didn't tell the police about the briefcase, and they're waiting for your next move."

"Why? What do they expect me to do if not go to the police?"

"Make a run for it with their cash."

"I'd never!"

"I know, you're a law-abiding citizen."

She drew herself up with a sniff. "You make that sound like a crime."

"Not a crime. Just predictable." He snapped open the case and pulled out a pack of bills nearly as thick as his fist. "Haven't you ever wondered what it would be like to have this much money?"

She moved one shoulder in nonchalant acceptance, but her eyes danced with dreams and maybes. "Who hasn't?"

"But how many of us would just take it if we found it?"

She bit her lip as he fanned the wad at her.

"We'd all be tempted," he admitted, "but I like to think most of us have a conscience. We'd worry about the poor sap who'd lost his wallet."

"This is more than a wallet."

"Exactly," he agreed. "All the more reason for any intelligent citizen to not attempt to keep it."

"Because the possibility of some type of illegal activity is obvious?"

"That and because anyone who has this much money to lose could cause a person a world of hurt. Money is power," he suggested, running the bills through his fingers again. "Yet this amount of cash is tempting. Someone might like to be rewarded for finding it."

She reached out to snatch the pack out of his hands and put it back in the case. "Your point?" she asked, snapping the locks shut.

"You deserve something for saving their booty and for not turning it over to the cops."

Her mouth fell open. "Are you crazy?"

"Nope," he assured her. "It's going to be your reason for keeping it when they ask."

"That makes me sound crooked!"

"Which is exactly what you're going to pretend to be—if you want to find out who this money belongs to." He shrugged. "But it could be a little risky. You might just want to turn it over to the police. They'd take and have it locked up in the evidence locker until someone comes forward to claim it."

"You know, that'll never happen," she protested.

"I know, but do you? Are you going to let whoever's behind this get away?"

If he'd waved a red flag in front of her, it couldn't have worked better, and he swallowed his grin as she drew herself up to what he judged to be her full five foot seven height, in heels, to meet his stare head on. "Just how do we set this trap?"

"Very carefully. And we start by your going home. With this," he said and reached out to tap the case. "And I'll go with you."

"Wait a minute. Why do you have to come?"

"Protection, remember?" he reminded her, but she wasn't willing to admit she needed him. He could see it in her face. Yet she knew what he did. Drug dealers, if that's who was involved in the switch, weren't nice people, and their hired help would be a lot leaner and meaner than Bill Zaworski.

That limited her options, and on examination, he was going to come up as the lesser of two evils. Regardless, she remained reluctant to let him a little bit farther into her life, and being a curious type of guy, he had to wonder why.

During the year they'd been together, she'd remained careful about holding him at arm's length. The only interaction between them was professional, nothing personal. No family information was ever exchanged, no elaborations on weekend plans, nothing more threatening than a few opinions and casual or overheard comments.

For himself, it wasn't that he wasn't interested in what she did, where she went or who she was, it was only respect for the space she obviously wanted to maintain between them. She kept things strictly business with him as her co-tenant, and he didn't push or rebel against her decision. They were, after all, partners of sorts.

Of course, that hadn't stopped him from the occasional wayward thought. What would it take to crack the cool shell she encased herself in? A simple kiss, an all out seduction? But musings had never given way to any attempt to satisfy his curiosity, and they never would. The arrangement they had was perfect. He wasn't going to blow it on a whim.

Still he remained willing, if she ever gave the signal, to follow her lead. She might believe, and want him to believe, that she was oblivious to him as anything more than another professional, but he knew better. She could refuse to acknowledge the pull of man and woman that constantly surged between them like a resilient undertow, but that didn't mean it wasn't there waiting to suck them under at the first opportunity.

That was, perhaps, why she continued to hesitate while he watched her. Even when her life could depend on her asking for his company, she knew what could be between them if she ever opened the gate. Or, maybe, it wasn't him she was afraid of. It could be she had other reasons for being reluctant to allow him closer.

It was only an impression, but from a comment here, an innuendo there, it was clear she didn't trust men. Why he couldn't be sure, and if tempted to dig around to find out why she was anti-testosterone, he had ethics. He didn't delve into someone's background unless invited—and paid.

Besides, she wasn't really his type. Cool, controlled, dedicated. All were symptoms of a woman who liked commitment, and he wasn't ready or willing to give one. Didn't think he ever would be. Not with his past or his future. And he wasn't ready to ruin a good working relationship to take part in a fleeting personal one even if it could be gratifying.

"What's wrong, Chris?" he finally prompted when she remained uncertain and silent, determined to get deeper into her life whether she wanted him in it or not—at least on this case. "Afraid to be alone with me?"

Her chin came up. "No, I'm not. But before we go, I have to get some work done."

"So do I," he agreed and shoved away from the desk. He was willing and able to give her some room and some control of the situation. "Just let me know when you're ready."

"Sure," she agreed, but as he strolled casually out of her office, Christine wasn't sure she'd ever be ready to go home again. Not if he would be riding along with her.

He disappeared, and she sank into her chair once more to cradle her pounding head in her hand. She didn't know how a day that had started out so bright and sunny had turned into such a fog-enshrouded trial, but it had. And it didn't look like it was going to get any better any time soon.

Her gaze drifted to the briefcase still sitting next to her "in" box and glared at it. If the right person had picked it up instead of her, she wouldn't be faced with taking a man home with her. She nearly groaned. Not just *a* man. David.

She grimaced, and the ache in her skull worsened. Him in her home. She couldn't imagine it. Didn't want to think about it, but she did. And the image wasn't all bad. Not when somebody somewhere was going to be knocking on her door looking for the money she'd taken—through no fault of her own.

Sighing, she reached for the folder on the top of the pile she'd brought in with her earlier. Like it or not, she was going to feel a lot safer with him nearby than if she was sitting alone waiting for what appeared to be the inevitable. He'd certainly saved her from Bill Zaworski earlier. Without him in the office, she'd probably be in the hospital. Or worse.

Shivering against the thought, she tried to force herself to concentrate, but even with her head down, she could see the briefcase out of the corner of her eye. It made her mind wander, and the folder, open before her, remained unread as she stared at the leather attaché.

What did the money represent? Could it possibly be legitimate? It didn't seem likely. No one withdrew from a bank and carried around that kind of cash for any reasonable expense or transaction. Such withdrawals were usually used for exchanges that nobody wanted traced. That meant the odds were better than even the briefcase had been in the courthouse for some type of illegitimate enterprise.

She frowned and unconsciously tapped out a quiet beat on the desk with the pencil she was holding. Could it be drug money as David suggested? Or was it only as simple as a bribe?

A bribe would be safer, less threatening somehow, and yet it was worse. That would mean one of her colleagues was on the take, accepting payment instead of insuring justice was served. That didn't sit well, but what could she do about it?

David wanted to set a trap. He saw that as the only way to find out who the money belonged to. But was it? She brought her hand up to rest her chin in her palm as she stared at the brown case.

She would have preferred turning the attaché over to the police. Investigating illegal activity was their job, not hers. She and the others in her occupation simply defended the innocent and prosecuted the guilty, but David was probably right about turning the money over to the authorities. The end result would only lead to a dead end. Or would it? Her eyes narrowed as she considered.

If the police had the briefcase, they would dust for fingerprints and maybe try to trace the numbers of the bills. She heaved a sigh of frustration. The fingerprints would probably be those of some unknown underling, a courier, and the cash wasn't bank wrapped nor did it consist of nicely pressed, unwrinkled bills. The money was randomly bundled and well used. Not traceable.

She scowled fiercely, arguing the case in her head. The attaché itself was of little investigative value. It was a common style and could be bought in several places she could think of off the top of her head. No product from an exclusive shop, it would prove untraceable, too, and would leave the police with nothing to go on.

Yet she suddenly realized she was only looking at the situation from one angle. The outside. Standing, leaving the folder where it lay, she dropped her pencil and stood to open the attaché. Inside could be answers.

Removing the money, one pack at a time, she searched but found nothing. The case held no clues, no handwritten instructions, no indication of the owner, of where the money was coming from or going to.

Forced to admit defeat, she repacked and closed the case once more before pausing to stand, chewing at her lower lip in contemplation.

If she, or anyone else, wanted to know who the money belonged to, the police definitely weren't the answer. Without some clues or a lead to follow, any investigation launched would die a quick death, and the attaché would end up sitting on a shelf—where it would likely remain indefinitely. Or at least until some judge, after a statutory number of years, ruled it belonged to the state. That meant nobody would ever know where the bills had come from or why. And she didn't like that option.

Somebody in the city was carrying out illegal activity in a court of law. She didn't know who, but she wanted to. And the only way to find out was to do what David said. Set a trap.

Her stomach rolled uneasily. She was going to have to trust David. Not that trust was a problem. With his law enforcement background, with the work she'd seen him accomplish, she couldn't doubt he knew what he was doing. On regular cases anyway. A briefcase full of money was hardly the norm.

Her stomach rolled again. By agreeing to his strategy, she just hoped that he, and she with him, weren't biting off more than they could chew. He might be ready for and enjoy the mystery of unraveling a conspiracy, but she preferred the slow and calculated pace of the legal system. And she liked to work alone. Or at least without men.

She sat once more, setting the case on the floor beside her and picking up her pencil again.

It was a personal prejudice. Her feelings against men. Born in her youth while under the restraints set by a father who had controlled the lives of everyone in the family, her feelings weren't due to abuse. She couldn't remember her father ever striking her, her mother or her sister, but her memories were filled with the oppression of his word as law.

As a child, as a young girl, as a teenager, she'd never had any decision-making power. Only he ruled. He was the one with the authority, and always in charge, his judgments never took into account the opinions or wishes of others. Too wrapped up in his own desires, not once could she remember him ever considering the possibility that his dictates were wrong for everyone else but him.

Christine silently shook her head. She knew she was wrong to compare every man to her father, but she'd seen his image too often in others. Yet never in David.

Since the time they'd met and become office mates, any decisions about the space they shared, about the employment of the twins, had been made jointly and through calm, intelligent discussion. He never tried to force his opinion on her or insist his way was better. He listened to her just as she listened to him. That was why she trusted him and his judgment and why she was going to go along with him and his plans for the briefcase.

He had been a police officer once, and his private investigator's license allowed him to continue in his chosen profession without benefit of uniform or badge. He knew what he was doing, and what they were getting into. She hoped.

Sighing, she bent over the folder, determined to get the work that needed doing done, and Mandy helped still her restless thoughts by interrupting with a phone call from Patty Zaworski.

The woman was sobbing—with gratitude and with guilt at her husband's arrest. It took the better part of half an hour for Christine to soothe away feelings of betrayal for the man who had fathered her children, but by the time the conversation ended, Patty was more upbeat and Christine was able to focus on her work with a sense of satisfaction.

If the ache in her head persisted, it was neglected and ignored as she tackled one problem after another. And absorbed in dictating letters of settlement, inquiry and denial, lunch hour came and went without notice. Still it was the brief that took time.

It needed to be edited down and filed by the end of the week, and that process provided the perfect, if unacknowledged, excuse not to go home to the unknown with a man she was just realizing she barely knew. Yet if he didn't push her, didn't insist on her immediate attention to the disposal of the attaché, he didn't go away either.

"You know, if you took some more aspirin, your head might stop hurting."

It took a moment for his words to break through the chaos of legal phrases and rhetoric running through her mind, but when they did, she looked up to find him standing in the door.

"You're rubbing your forehead," he told her, forcing her to focus on what he'd said.

"Oh." Suddenly self-conscious, she tucked the offending appendage out of sight on her lap, but he didn't leave. He remained where he was, watching her, waiting, and she quickly looked to the clock on the wall. "It's past five o'clock."

"The twins are gone. We should be, too."

Reminded, her eyes dropped to the briefcase beside her chair on the floor, and he seemed to read her mind as fear coiled into a tight ball inside her stomach.

"You don't have to do this," he told her quietly. "I'd like you to, but it's your decision. This could be dangerous. We don't know who we're dealing with."

Oddly, his warning and his honesty encouraged rather than discouraged her from doing what she wanted to avoid. "No, you're right. The police can't do this one alone. We have to help."

His smile was entirely too appreciative, and she turned quickly from it and him to begin gathering her purse and the briefcase. "You'll follow me home?"

"In a manner of speaking."

Frowning, she slowly approached him, clutching the case between them. "I don't understand."

"It wouldn't do for them to realize we're working together. Just remember that if you can't see me, it doesn't mean I'm not there."

Stopping before him, suddenly it wasn't so simple any more. The idea of setting a trap, catching the crooks, bringing them to justice. A million things could go wrong in the process, and the possibilities of what could happen hit her hard.

They weren't playing a game. The people the cash belonged to could be deadly, but in defiance of her own fear, she lifted her chin to combat her own turmoil. She wasn't going to cut and run. After all, bullies were her favorite opponent. "So what's the plan?"

The approval in his gaze helped wipe away any anxiety when he shrugged. "You go to the garage, get in your car and drive home. I'll meet you there."

"You'll need the address..."

"I have it," he assured her. "I got it from Candy."

"Did you tell her why?"

"No, I didn't want to get the twins involved in this." He turned to lead the way out of the room. "I let her draw her own conclusions."

Stifling a moan, Christine shut off her office lights and followed him, trying not to imagine what speculation he had just created between the two sister secretaries. Hopes of romantic intrigue in the office between their two bosses?

"I'll leave first," he told her, walking to the front door. "Wait a few minutes then go straight to your car and home. No stops, no detours. And take your time. Just act normal."

Normal. As he slipped out into the hall and left her alone, she wasn't sure what that was any more, but she wanted to when, following in his footsteps the required few minutes later, the corridor proved to be darker than she remembered. It also, unexpectedly, had way too many places for someone to hide.

Hurrying, she noticed the quiet as well. With the five o'clock rush already come and gone, it was very quiet in the endless passageway. But it, at least, wasn't as bad as the underground garage.

When the elevator stopped and the doors slid open in the basement, silence greeted her. Silence and an infinite stretch of cement. The cold, gray pavement wove around a maze of pillars, shadows and automobiles, and to her way of thinking, it was the perfect place for a "snatch and grab."

Swallowing, it took all of her willpower to step out of the car and onto the concrete. And it took considerable restraint not to run—straight for her Honda that, parked in its usual space, was much farther away than she would have liked.

Remembering David's caution, sure he was somewhere close by, she tried not to rush, and she didn't look around as she walked. Still it was difficult, nearly impossible, to stop herself from glancing over her shoulder. Yet she managed. Barely. By concentrating on the hollow ring of her footsteps echoing from wall to wall.

The lonely sound was reassuring because it gave testimony to her solitude. No one was following her. No one was creeping up from behind. Still she felt a presence. Somebody watching her. Was it David? Or was it someone else?

Tightening her grip on the briefcase, she covered the remaining distance to her Honda with a few quick strides, and fumbling to get her keys in the lock, tried to discreetly eye the black-glassed van and the other vehicles waiting nearby.

Deserted, and apparently empty, they stood motionless between the chipped yellow lines of their allotted spaces. But were they what they appeared? Unoccupied? Or was somebody sitting, observing, inside?

Finally, the key turned, and she threw herself into the driver's seat. Immediately she slammed and relocked the door, but no one tried to follow her into the vehicle. If her heart was pounding, if she was braced for the worst, the building remained still around her. She was safe. Or seemed to be.

Quickly starting the engine nevertheless, she pointed her car for the daylight waiting beyond the garage, and eagerly escaped into the sun's dying rays. Outside of the confines of the basement parking lot, she felt better, but the ordeal wasn't over. It was just beginning, and the briefcase sitting on the seat beside her was a constant reminder of what could lay ahead.

Usually she looked forward to going home at the end of the day, but the approaching evening didn't promise to be a quiet or relaxing one. Not when she was expecting company of an unknown origin.

Glancing at the attaché when she stopped at a light, her teeth worried her lower lip. The case looked like hers but wasn't. What was inside should belong to her but didn't. What it contained was something that she, perhaps, had dreamed of having. Money. And a lot of it. Yet this particular batch of bills was something she wanted no part of because, while money was supposed to buy anything, the only thing the cash she was carrying would buy was trouble.

Shivering as a chill shuddered down her spine, she looked away from the leather case to her rear view mirror in search of David and reassurance, but she didn't see him in the traffic behind her. She didn't even know what kind of car he drove. Yet he was with her. He had given her his promise, and she believed him. It might seem as if she was by herself, but she wasn't. He was with her. And visible or invisible, his presence was calming.

The light turned green, and she moved forward again toward The Bunker Hill Towers. The buildings weren't far away. Not as driving in L.A. went. Her commute compared to the drive endured by some who worked in the City of Angels was insignificant. A few miles rather than a few hours, but the Towers were perfect for her.

They might not be on the beach or in the hills that most residents of Los Angeles County seemed to prefer, but they were close to the courthouse, to the office and to where all the action she needed to partake in was. However, pulling into the driveway and entering the dark walls of another parking garage, the name of her residence suddenly gave her pause. She hoped that living in a place named after a battle from the American Revolution wasn't prophetic.

Fortunately, no guns were aimed or blazing when she got to her allotted parking spot and, thankfully, the line of fire was crowded. Other people from the complex, many who she recognized, were present when she got out of her car. Along with her, they were headed for the elevator and their front doors, and that was fine with her. She liked having company for the ride to her floor because safety could be found in numbers. Yet the numbers dwindled at each stop. By the time she stepped out into the carpeted corridor leading to her place, she was alone once more.

Never having realized how quiet it was inside the complex, the silence pressed in on her as she hurried down the hall past forbidding nooks and crannies she'd never even noticed before.

Half expecting and half hoping David was concealed in one of them, she was disappointed he wasn't. When she reached her door, he still wasn't with her, but he was nearby. She was sure of it. Probably right behind her, "watching her back" as it were.

Glancing anxiously over her shoulder for some sign of him, she tried to put the key in the lock. Tried because she couldn't seem to keep hold of the ring. She dropped it twice before finally getting the key where it needed to go.

When the bolt turned, she didn't need any encouragement to enter. She shoved inside, anxious for sanctuary, but yanking the key free from the lock, she looked up and down the hall one last time.

David wasn't in sight. No one was. Not friend or foe. She was by herself. At least for the moment.

Swiftly shutting the door, she twisted the bolt back into place and struggled with the security chain. It wasn't cooperative. Not when her fingers were shaking, but somehow, she rattled it into its socket—and immediately heaved a sigh of relief.

The sound almost made her laugh out loud at her own sense of melodrama. Yet behind the closed door, safety was an illusion. She felt secure, but when she turned around, a shadow was waiting. A shadow that was bigger than she was, and its voice came to her with a smile.

"I've been waiting for you."

Chapter 3

DAVID HEARD the gasp, knew what it meant and leapt forward to wrap his hand over her mouth to silence the scream. "For Pete's sake, don't yell! You'll have the whole building down on top of us!"

Her response was blunt. Her elbow connected sharply with his ribs.

He let her go with a hiss.

"You scared the hell out of me!" she accused, rounding on him with an indignant huff.

And he had. He could see it in her eyes, in the way her breath had her breasts rapidly falling and rising beneath her business suit, but he wasn't very sympathetic. "Yeah, well, you should have been here a few minutes ago. The yowl I was greeted with by that thing you call a pet nearly cost it one of its nine lives."

"Arthur! Did you hurt Arthur?"

David rapidly threw his hands up in self-defense to avoid the attack she was obviously prepared to launch in defense of her cat. "No, but if he howls like that again, I won't be responsible for my actions."

Fumbling for a switch in the darkened hall, she scowled at him as the lights came on. "He was only protecting his territory."

"He could do it more quietly," David grumbled and earned a glare.

"It'll be hours now before he comes out."

"Sorry." But he wasn't. The damn cat had nearly given him a heart attack. He watched her look around the hallway, for her pet or something else, he wasn't sure.

"How did you get in here?"

Unwilling to give up trade secrets that he knew she wouldn't approve of, he shrugged. "Does it matter?"

"I thought you were ethical."

"I thought you wanted to be protected," he countered, and he was doing his best.

During the day, he'd had a friend, an off-duty police officer, keep an eye on her condo. No one had come near it. And while she'd been wrapped up working in her office, he'd left his briefly to move his car closer to hers. That had given him the chance to check out the garage just moments before she'd had to walk through it, but she didn't have to know that. Only he did because he was the one who was responsible for keeping her safe—and for convincing her to take part in a charade that's ending was uncertain.

"I pulled the curtains," he continued. "That's why it's so dark in here."

"Made yourself at home, did you?" she asked sweetly, but her smile wasn't friendly and her arched eyebrow was suspicious.

Unimpressed by her wrath, he let his own lips curve. "Made sure no one else was in here waiting for you."

She blinked. The reminder was blunt but necessary. He wasn't with her to keep her company.

"I brought dinner," he said, in way of offering peace and gestured past her to the white bags sitting on her kitchen counter. "I figured you might not have enough to feed two." He shrugged. "I hope you like Chinese."

The eyebrow arched again. "Did you get sweet and sour sauce?"

"Plenty of extra," he confirmed and found himself admiring her style. He'd scared her, forced her to remember it was no game they were playing, but she wasn't crumbling under the strain. She might be nervous, probably even frightened of what lay ahead, but she wasn't going to show it. Not to him. Maybe not even to herself. He appreciated that. The lady had guts. "How about we eat while it's still luke warm?"

"I could be convinced."

She led the way to the dining room and the table set neatly in its center where she left her purse and the briefcase while he brought the white bags packed with food.

"How about some wine?" she asked.

"Better than water," he accepted and, glancing around, took a seat as she disappeared into the kitchen to find it.

His initial search in the dark had revealed few details about the place she lived, but with the lights on and the fading sun sneaking in between cracks in the blinds and curtains, he could clearly see what she had filling the rooms.

Her place was classy. Like her. The pillows matched the couch, blended with the carpet and accented the paintings on the walls. He figured that meant she had taste. Which was more than he did. Or at least more than he knew he had, but then he'd never wasted a lot of time trying to figure out if his furniture was part of a matched set. If he had a bed to sleep in and a chair to sit on, he was happy, but she needed more.

It showed in the decor, in the careful placement of knick knacks and bric-a-brac, and in the precise mood the colors and placement of couch and table created. She didn't just live in her condo. It was her home. It was something she took pride in, something that reflected her personality and her preferences, and it was somewhere she could relax. Even if she wasn't totally at ease with him in it with her. Him and a bag full of money. But he'd been with nervous clients before.

"Nice digs," he told her, accepting a fluted glass of white wine when she returned from the kitchen. "And convenient."

"That's why I picked it," she agreed and left again only to reappear seconds later with china plates and silverware. "I'm close to everywhere I need to go."

"And far from the gridlock on the freeway."

"It lets me sleep later," she admitted, and he grinned, trying to picture her in bed and immediately wished he hadn't.

She would look different when just waking up. The makeup would be gone, the hair would be tousled rather than carefully combed and styled, and her clothes. He quickly shoveled a helping of rice into his mouth to help clear the lump that had formed in his throat, and cursed himself silently.

She wasn't his type. Cool, analytical and blond. His style was more hot, athletic and brunette. Besides, he wasn't with her to stage a seduction but to offer protection. Yet the curiosity remained. About her. About who she was behind the mask she always wore.

Grabbing a chicken wing, he studied her across the table. "Tell me about yourself."

If he'd fired a bullet over her head, the alarm that flared in her eyes couldn't have expressed more terror, and she immediately attempted a hasty retreat. "I'm not very interesting. What about you?"

Intrigued by her need to hide behind anonymity, he moved his shoulders indifferently. He was willing to go along with her evasion. At least for the moment. His questions, and her answers, could come later. "I'm the only son of an insurance agent and his wife, but I'm not the only child. I have three sisters."

"Three?" she repeated in surprise.

"All older," he confirmed and sipped his wine. "I'm the baby of the family."

She hid, what he was sure was a smile, behind her own glass. "And they all live here in L.A.?"

"No, my folks are in San Diego, and my sisters are spread around the area."

She set her glass down, breaking eye contact with him. "If your sisters are older, can I assume they're married?"

"Two of them are," he agreed. "And both have kids."

"You're a proud uncle?"

"Three times over, and my sisters hate me to visit. They complain I spoil my nieces and nephew."

Her smile transformed her face. It made her look younger, more accessible, and it was hard to look away. He managed only by grabbing another chicken wing.

"What about your other sister?" she prodded, using the chop sticks provided by the restaurant like an old pro instead of the fork she'd set beside her plate. "If she's not married, she must be a career woman then."

"She's a cop in Santa Barbara."

Christine frowned. "Why so far away?"

"She wanted to escape the big city."

"Santa Barbara isn't exactly small."

"But it's not like L.A. either."

She conceded the point with a nod. "What about you?"

"What about me?"

"You're not married."

"No, but I was."

"I'm sorry."

Her apology was quick, but the sting of the wound had healed years before. All that remained was the regret for something precious lost, and he shrugged his acceptance of that lingering hurt, knowing it wasn't a mistake he'd make again. "Don't be. Police work is hard on wives."

"Men, too, I think," she suggested softly.

Looking up to catch her studying his face, he grimaced in mock pain. "Ah, I see you've noticed my eye patch."

She leaned forward, putting her elbows on the table, and her blue gaze filled with sympathy. It was an emotion he still hated and resented but, of necessity, had learned to deal with. "It happened while you were on duty?"

"About a year before you and I met."

"A year?" she asked, obviously surprised. "I thought you'd just been starting out as a private investigator when we got together. You must have been working at it for awhile then?"

"No," he denied. "In between being hurt and setting up the office I've got now, I was basically laying around doing nothing but feeling sorry for myself."

Her mouth fell open, his confession shocking. Or amazing. He wasn't sure which, and she didn't seem to be able to make up her mind either. She stammered before speaking again. "It must have been hard."

He nodded, but hard didn't describe it. Not for him. The pain, the shock, the denial, the loss of self-esteem. And the placement on disability at the age of twenty-seven. That had nearly destroyed him.

On discharge from the hospital, he'd grabbed hold of a whiskey bottle and hadn't let go for a month, but if he'd been ready to quit, his family hadn't. And neither had his friends. The other cops, his comrades, had made it clear that being scarred wasn't the end of life.

Yet he wasn't ready to tell her that. Not when the memories were all still too fresh and when his emotions on the subject remained, at times, raw and at others unclear. Discarding the chicken wing he'd been gnawing on, he looked away from the interested light shining in her eyes and side-stepped to a safer area of discussion. "It was harder losing my dream."

"Your dream?"

"Of being a cop," he explained. "I was working on becoming a detective. I was going to be the next Joe Friday."

She burst out laughing, and he stared in surprise.

It wasn't that he was offended. Rather, he was intrigued. By her, by the woman behind the persona of Christine Dunn, Attorney-at-Law. She was a stranger. A beautiful stranger, and without the professional cloak she usually kept pulled tightly around her, she was mesmerizing. He leaned forward, putting an elbow on the table, too. "What? You have a problem with someone who wants to uphold the law?"

"No, it's just," she managed, obviously struggling to hide her mirth with decorum. It wasn't, after all, polite to laugh at guests, but he enjoyed watching the battle as she gestured futilely and tried to finish her sentence. "It's just that he's so...lifeless!"

David grinned at the accurate malignment of the monotone-speaking, straight-faced hero detective of television's *Dragnet*.

She leaned closer. "I see you as more of a *Miami Vice* kind of cop."

"I think that's a compliment," he murmured and, looking into her eyes, was shocked by the sudden snap of electricity.

It jumped from him to her. Stunning, paralyzing, arousing. It startled the laughter from her eyes, put high color in her cheeks and abruptly had her diving back into the rice and chicken set out on the plate before her.

"So why did you decide to stay in L.A. when your sister when to Santa Barbara?" she asked, keeping her head down.

Carefully setting aside the delicate glass he was holding, afraid the stem would be cracked by the gut-clenching heat that had just jolted through his body, he sat back in his chair. "Because L.A. has so many more interesting personalities."

"A peculiar choice of adjectives to describe the L.A. police force's clientele," she observed, keeping her focus on the food before her.

"But accurate," he assured her with a sigh that didn't escape her notice.

Her gaze came back up to his. "You miss it."

"It's what I was trained for, what I always wanted to be and do—go out and get the bad guys."

She bit her lower lip. "I was less ambitious. I just wanted to make sure they went to jail."

"Something the police appreciate," he assured her.

She shook her head. "Some of them maybe. Others don't like attorneys, and there are some who have made it clear they think lawyers are on the wrong side of justice."

"Every profession has members whose actions reflect badly on the rest."

She wrinkled her nose. "I think the legal profession has more than a few."

Wiping his hands on a napkin, he studied her. "If you feel that way, why did you choose to become an attorney then?"

"Because it felt right and because I liked the idea of helping people obtain what's legally theirs."

He grimaced and tossed the napkin aside. "But all those years of cracking the books..."

"Law school was the best," she insisted. "The people, the debates, the camaraderie."

"The exams."

She laughed again, the sound shivering over his skin and stimulating hormones that had him sitting straighter, but she was unaware of her effect on him. She was oblivious to the desire rocketing through his system, but he thought that was okay. At least until he could figure out what he should, could, or wanted to do about it. Or if she'd even let him try.

"We used to stay up to the wee hours arguing case law," she told him with a heartfelt sigh. "It was amazing. Wonderful." Her smile lingered. "Losing our little group, watching it break up and scatter across the country, was the worst part of graduation."

"Sounds like family."

"It was better than family," she denied, unexpected anger creeping into her voice. "We belonged, we shared. We respected each other's opinions."

He said nothing as she jumped up to start carrying dishes back to the kitchen, but his interest was piqued. The lady had depths, and wounds, that she kept under tight wrap. But he was good at ferreting out what others hid. Grabbing his own plate, he followed her into the room that was fitted with every modern appliance known to man and that had counters and an island as immaculate as the rest of her home. "Your parents came to your graduation?"

At the sink, she didn't turn to face him. "Of course not."

He added his plate to hers in the sink and lingered to enjoy the subtle scent of her perfume. "I take it you're not close to them."

"No, I'm not," she agreed, shutting off the water. "We don't see things the same way."

"But they must be proud of you," he pressed gently because even in profile, he could see the pain in her expression.

"I really don't know what they think," she denied and shook her head. "And I don't know where they are. Last time I heard they were in Maryland."

"They travel a lot?"

"They never stop."

The bitterness was there. The loneliness, and suddenly he understood the neatness of her home, the care she gave it. "It must have been interesting seeing the country as a kid."

"It was interesting if you were on the outside looking in," she agreed dully. "Never knowing from one year to the next if you'd be at the same school. Never being able to make any real friends."

"Your father or mother must have had a job that saw them transfer a lot."

Her laughter came without humor. "It wasn't a job that made him keep uprooting us. It was an ad in a magazine or the want for warmer weather or maybe just because he was bored."

The picture she painted wasn't happy. Her childhood had been hard and lonely, but he knew of one thing that could have eased the insecurity. "Did you have any brothers or sisters?"

"A sister. I just heard from her..." Glancing up to find him watching her, Christine's sudden smile faltered, and she abruptly stiffened. "When do you think the call will come?"

The clang of the invisible door slamming shut between them was nearly deafening, and if David wanted to open it again, he didn't make the attempt. Instead, curbing his investigative instincts, his own curiosity, and respecting her privacy, he answered her with a noncommittal grunt. "Depends on how far they are in checking you out."

"What?"

"They'll want to know who they're dealing with," he explained, ready and willing to distract her from the personal pain darkening her soul because he understood the need to avoid to conquer. "So you can bet they're asking questions."

"About me?"

He nodded, and she stammered.

"Who are they asking?"

"Anyone they can think of, but they'll be subtle," he assured her soberly, leaning back against the counter and crossing his arms over his chest. "They won't be telling anybody why they want to know or that you're walking around with a suitcase of cash that isn't yours."

"How comforting," she fumed, but he ignored her sarcasm.

"And, of course, they're still watching, waiting to see if, now that you're home, you'll pack and take off for the airport."

"Not likely," she grumbled, remembering the shadows in the garage.

"Once they're sure that you're staying put, they'll call."

She bit her lip. "You're talking hours."

"At least," he agreed. "We might be spending the whole night together."

"The whole night!" Panic clogged her throat. Him in her house, with her alone, until the sun came up. She swallowed and blinked away sudden intimate images of him, in bed, asleep, with her. "You can't be serious."

He winked. "What's the matter? Don't you think you can keep your hands off me?"

Mortified that he seemed to have read her mind, heat rushed into her cheeks, but she held onto her composure and tried to level him with a glare. "You should be so lucky."

"You'd be the lucky one," he grinned and pointed to her feet. "You might as well get comfortable. Take off your shoes. Every woman I know likes to shed shoes, pantyhose and bra when they get home, and I don't want to stop you from doing what comes natural. After all, there's no need to be formal just because I'm here."

She sputtered, and her toes protested. She'd been wanting to kick off her pumps since she'd walked in the door, but she'd resisted because of him and in the hope that he wouldn't be with her long.

He shoved off from the counter. "This is your home. You just do what you usually do and pretend I'm not here."

Clenching her teeth, she wished it was going to be that easy, making believe he wasn't with her, and temper igniting as he strolled out of the room as if he hadn't a care in the world, she abruptly determined it was going to be.

Simply because he could make her kitchen smaller just by standing in it didn't mean she had to let him intimidate her. He was just a man. An attractive man, maybe, but he wasn't with her because he wanted to be. He was in her home because she was the proud owner of a briefcase full of money she wanted to get rid of.

Reaching down, she yanked off her shoes. He was right. She didn't need to impress him by dress or manner. The two of them weren't on a date, and she wasn't going to act like she was. Not that she'd been on such a social outing in some time, and he was reminding her why.

Arrogance. He was full of it. Like most men. He, being one of them, was so sure he knew what she wanted, like remove her shoes—and leap into bed with him. Typical. The male ego. It was always the largest part of any man. She shook her head. And to think, for a few minutes, she'd actually thought he was different.

Squaring her shoulders, she headed for the door, her bedroom and her cat. David could fend for himself and do without her. It was certain she would easily do without him. She didn't need a man to keep her company, to escort her, to entertain her, to dream about. Because the kind of relationship she wanted didn't exist. One where a man and a woman were on equal terms.

Still sometimes she wished for it, usually when she was tired—as she was at the moment.

Marching into her bedroom, she reminded herself that such a thing just wasn't possible. Not for her. That was why she remained, and why she preferred to be, alone.

THE ATTACK came out of nowhere.

He wasn't expecting it. He wasn't prepared. And David groaned in his sleep as the blackness parted and the demon from his past stepped into his nightmare with machete in hand.

The routine patrol he and his partner had been on was going from bad to worse, and the back up they'd called for was still nowhere in sight.

The other squads were on the way. Help was coming. The problem was, he and Randy were no longer at the drug house. They were in pursuit of suspects—something the other cops coming in wouldn't know until they reached the scene and found at least one person laying on the front porch dying.

That was why ambulances were running in, too. With the way bullets had been flying, more than one van would be needed to carry the injured and wounded away.

Racing down another alley and across a dark street, David thought it a miracle he didn't need one himself. He or Randy. But, thankfully, neither he nor his partner had been injured in the gun fight over drugs and money. At least not yet.

Leaping over a discarded garbage can and the refuse pouring from it, he knew it was too soon to count his blessings. The night was young, and the battle wasn't over. It was simply continuing on another front.

A few feet ahead someone abruptly stepped out of the shadows. David slid to a halt beside Randy and felt his blood run cold.

The light from the full moon overhead glinted off sharp steel. The machete in the kid's hand was long and deadly, and the smile of welcome on his face warning because he wasn't alone. He had friends.

David reached out to grab Randy's arm beside him, to stop him from moving forward, but it wasn't necessary. Randy saw what he did, and as one, they immediately started backing up from the half circle of bodies forming in front of them. But a sound to the rear had them turning. The other half of the circle was closing in behind them.

David muttered against his dream, and the terror, as he and Randy went back-to-back. They were surrounded. Outnumbered. Alone.

Holding his service revolver firmly in his right hand, David counted the odds at roughly five-to-one and fought disbelief. They'd only been chasing three. Three fleeing street kids. But the trio were obviously part of a gang. One of many in the city that, in total, numbered some fifty thousand members, and this particular band was ready to fight and defend its territory and its members.

In his sleep, David murmured, warning the boys who ranged from thirteen to twenty back, but they kept coming forward, tightening the circle. Randy tried, too. He did what he could to convince them nobody wanted to die, nobody else needed to be hurt, but the boys didn't care. On drugs, on a power high, they merely paused, then charged as one.

David's body jerked as the memory of the gun kicking in his hand made him jump, swear and yell as a screaming maniac wielding a two-foot piece of metal took a swing at his head.

He ducked, dodged, tried to fire again, but his gun was empty. Bodies were laying in the way when he tried to move. Yet the attack continued. Hand-to-hand as groans mixed with the wail of approaching sirens.

Behind him, he heard Randy cry out, but David couldn't help him. He was too busy holding off a side assault. He lurched to the left, recognizing too late that it was the wrong thing to do. The kid he was fighting was only a distraction, a decoy meant to draw him out and away so the teen with the machete had free aim.

David jumped, trying to avoid the blow, but he couldn't. He could only change the target. The machete hit him in the front, rather than the back, of the head.

He screamed agony, and somebody grabbed him.

"David! Wake up!"

Consciousness returned with a growl, and Christine cried out as his fingers closed with brutal intensity over her arms. But he didn't hear. Lost in another world, he shook her on a snarl that filled her with dread. He didn't know where he was, who she was, and in the faint light filtering through the curtains and with the patch over his eye, he looked like a pirate about to rip his enemy from stem to stern.

"David!"

Her desperate cry stopped him. It penetrated the fog, pierced the echo of fear holding him in the nightmare, and he blinked, stared and his fingers abruptly eased their hold. "Christine?"

"You were dreaming."

Cursing darkly, he pushed her from him, and kneeling next to the couch, she sat down hard on her backside as he swung his long legs from the sofa to the floor.

Silently rubbing her arms where he'd held so fiercely, she stayed out of the way as he shoved to his feet and began to pace. His gait was jerky. Angry. Each step was one of bitter fury.

Biting her lip, she waited for him to speak. To offer some type of explanation, but what could he say?

She didn't have to ask to know what he'd been dreaming about. The half coherent murmurs, the movements of distress as he'd thrashed on the couch. It had been the accident. The one that had robbed him of one eye and caused what must have been excruciating pain.

Lacing her fingers together in her lap, she remained kneeling on the floor in the robe she'd hastily thrown over her nightgown when his agony, and the anxious pawing of her cat, had wakened her. She bit her lip. At first she'd hesitated, unsure if she should wake him or not.

She hadn't wanted to invade his privacy, to make him aware of her witnessing his torment, but his suffering had been too much for her. It'd been impossible to stand by and do nothing. She'd had to try to free him of the ghosts, to remind him they were in the past, and to make him see he was safe.

Still, if she'd gotten through to him, if his restless strides were slowing and he was getting memory and himself under control, it was taking a major effort. His personal demons were strong and, she realized, the specters haunting him had yet to be put to rest.

Briefly, she debated leaving him alone to give him solitude to deal with a private hurt, but she couldn't. She knew what it was like to battle impotency alone and, as she hesitated, he finally stopped.

Standing with his legs spread in the night, his hands settled on his hips, and she could see the heave of his chest begin to ease. Yet if his ragged breathing was starting to quiet, watching him, her own breath unexpectedly caught in her throat.

To sleep, he'd stripped down to bare skin from the waist up, and in silhouette against the night, she could appreciate the width of his shoulders, the strength in his chest and recognize the dark hair scattered sparingly across his hard flesh. He made her mouth go dry. He filled her with long-buried desire.

Heart thudding heavily against her breast, she stared. With his head held high and his stance straight and proud, he reminded her of his name. Maverick. That wasn't only who he was, it was what he was.

Waging a quiet war with himself, making his way in life on a shadier side of law enforcement, he was like a wild stallion racing across the plains. Beautiful and free and fighting to remain in control of his own destiny.

She respected his endurance, his personal struggle, and she regretted the evening that had just passed. The hours spent alone in another room could have been spent instead in his company. He'd come to help her, but she'd ignored him, spurned him because he stirred in her things she didn't want to acknowledge much less feel. It was her loss, the time she could have enjoyed with him, and she wished she could get the night back.

"I'm sorry."

His words startled. Hoarse and honest, they scattered and echoed her own thoughts, and she shook her head in denial. "You don't have to apologize."

"I do. I woke you up," he sighed and raised a hand to drag it through the thickness of his hair that was already in disarray from the pillows on the couch.

"Actually, you didn't," she insisted. "Arthur did."

David's head came up. "Arthur?"

A white shadow appeared to brush her arm, and she pulled a cat into her lap. "Arthur. King Arthur, actually," she introduced cat to man. "He's very regal, and he came to get me when he thought you were in trouble."

"A noble cat?"

She could hear, if not see, the humor on his lips in the darkness filling the room. "Yes, and he's old. You probably nearly gave him a coronary when you snuck in here."

David grunted. "Yeah, well, it would have been a race to see which one of us went into cardiac arrest first."

She smiled. "He usually only yowls at other cats."

"Territorial," David quipped as she stroked the big white Tom. "He probably didn't like another man invading your space."

Very aware of the strange male who wasn't feline and who was standing half naked in her "space," she cleared her throat and slipped to her feet. "We'll let you get back to sleep now."

"I *am* sorry."

About to turn away, she shook her head. "You can't control your dreams."

"I wish I could control this one." Sighing again, he sank into a chair to drop his head in his hands, and the helplessness expressed in his action had her stepping forward to go to him, to offer help, comfort, but he stopped her.

"It's the first time in months that I've had it," he admitted, his voice quiet and raw with unspoken emotion. It made her feel guilty.

"It's probably my fault. I made you talk about it earlier."

"Maybe," he agreed and sat back to look at her across the shadows. "Your hair is loose."

His personal observation on her appearance had her self-consciously reaching up to touch the golden strands that she didn't know were reflecting like a halo in the muted light filtering into the room.

"You always wear it up at the office."

"It gets in the way," she said, backing up, dropping her hand and holding her cat between she and him like a shield. In the dark, plagued by too human nightmares, he didn't seem as strong, as able, and his vulnerability beckoned her to stay, but she didn't want to court disaster. David Maverick was the type of man every girl dreamed of. Even her.

Good looking, tall, dynamic, overpowering.

It was the latter that terrified her. She didn't want to be taken over. She wanted only to be part of a team. A partner to someone in life and love, but the authority in the unions she'd witnessed as a child and as an adult never seemed to be shared evenly. One of the pair always seemed to be in charge, and she was afraid it wouldn't be her.

"It's late," she told him.

"I won't wake you again."

She nodded silent acknowledgement but was reluctant to leave when his voice spoke of wounds not completely healed. "You're all right?"

"Fine. Go to bed."

It was an order, one she was ready and willing to obey. She wanted to escape. She needed to, but turning to go, the phone rang.

The sound was shrill. Unnaturally so. And it shot David to his feet even as it froze her where she stood. The money. How could she have forgotten?

"Our caller," he told her.

"It could be a wrong number," she denied, hoping it was as he moved toward the couch and the end table and the instrument as it rang again.

He turned on a lamp above it, making her blink and revealing to her equipment she hadn't noticed before. A box with wires was attached to the base of the phone, and it obviously belonged to him.

Staring at it, she wondered numbly what else he'd brought with him for the night that she hadn't seen, but he hit a button on the box to draw her attention and her gaze.

"Pick it up," he told her, "and talk naturally. We want a rendezvous and a reward."

Licking her lips, she moved forward to set the cat down and reached for the receiver while David mimicked her exact motions with another receiver connected to the box. "Hello?"

"Miss Dunn?" a male voice answered.

"Yes?"

"We've never met, but I believe you have something that belongs to me."

Chapter 4

"PERHAPS YOU can describe it for me, and I'll let you know if I do or not," Christine told the caller, and listening, David nodded approval with a wicked grin. She was playing it cool and lawyerly.

"A brown leather briefcase."

"Actually, I personally own such a case," she admitted and David almost hit her for dragging it out, but she only shrugged at his scowl.

"Yes, it appears I have yours. It has papers with your name on it."

Christine nodded. "And how do I know that the attaché I have is yours? I couldn't find any name on what was inside, except of course, those of a few presidents."

David smothered a sigh and bent to adjust the volume on the instrument recording the conversation. She was obviously determined to play this her way. He was just going to have to quietly go along for the ride, but if he wasn't totally amused by her antics, the person on the other end of the line was.

Laughter echoed jovially. "Yes, you're right, and I'm sure you're aware that each of them is dead."

The veiled threat had Christine's eyes darting to his, but David could only offer silent reassurance with a thumbs up sign to keep her going.

Licking her lips, she nodded acknowledgement to him and to the caller. "Yes, death is a natural end to life. It usually happens when you get old—like I'd like to be some day."

"Then perhaps we can arrange an exchange."

"Perhaps," she agreed after a slight hesitation, and the man on the other end of the line picked up on it immediately.

"Surely I don't have to convince you to return what isn't yours?"

"No, although the idea of keeping this particular find is tempting."

"But can you afford to pay for it?"

"No," she admitted with forthright honesty. "That's why I'm willing to return it. For a price."

Stunned silence echoed on the line.

"Or don't you feel that good workers should be rewarded?" she pressed, any alarm now hidden behind a deceptively calm expression.

"That depends," was the cautious response, and David nodded to her in approval and waved for her to continue.

"I did save you a lot of trouble," she told the caller. "In fact, I saved you all of your money. If I'd turned it over to the police, like a good lawyer should, I wonder how you would have gotten it back?"

"Point taken," came on a chuckle. "But I don't know that any lawyer's good."

She sighed. "A friend of mine was pointing out to me just today that a few can give the rest a bad name."

David shook his head and sank down again onto the chair. He didn't have to worry about her. She knew how to negotiate. It was a regular part of her job.

"What did you have in mind?"

"A small reward," she suggested, her fingers winding into the cord on the receiver and revealing to David the tension her face didn't show. "For my trouble and to get rid of some of those nagging bills I'm having some trouble paying. I've only a small practice, you know."

"Yes, we know," the voice agreed thoughtfully, and David saw Christine shiver.

Yet she said nothing as the silence stretched.

"How, exactly, would you define small?" the unknown voice finally asked.

Christine immediately swung to David, her eyes widening on him in question, but he only shrugged a non-committal response, leaving the figure up to her.

"I trust your judgment," she baited and held her breath.

"Perhaps one pack from the case?"

"I haven't counted, of course, but that seems fair."

"And the return of the rest?"

David hurriedly grabbed and scratched the word "public" on a pad and held it up to her.

"Some place public would be nice," she said, biting her lip before hastily elaborating. "Very public. Busy is best."

"A park?" came the question.

She wrinkled her nose as David shook his head. "Too Hollywood."

The laugh came again. "Why don't you pick then?"

David rapidly scribbled her a note once more, and she took it with a frown.

"Street corners are very busy downtown." She looked up at him, and he encouraged her to embellish with a gesture. "Intersections, crosswalks. Pedestrians everywhere. Who would notice if two people in a crowd happened to put their briefcases down at the same time?"

"You don't want to meet?"

"Anonymity has a nice ring, don't you think?" she returned airily, but her knuckles turned white as her fingers squeezed the telephone cord. "I don't know you, and you don't really want to know me."

"No looking right, no looking left?"

"That's best, don't you agree?"

David gave her a thumbs up and then jerked his finger across his neck in a sign to end the conversation as he handed her a final note with an intersection by the courthouse.

She repeated the names of the streets to the caller. "About eight o'clock tomorrow morning? Then we can both put this behind us."

"That would be preferable," the caller agreed. "You will be on time?"

"I'll be standing on the corner at precisely eight o'clock. I'll put the case down, totally intact except for my reward, lift a hand to brush my hair, and when I reach down again ..."

"You'll have *your* briefcase back."

"My secretary will be so pleased," Christine sighed. "Those briefs take so long to type."

And listening to her, David could almost believe she was totally relaxed. It was the way she was strangling the spiral wire running from the receiver to the base of the phone that convinced him she wasn't.

"Yes, we're just glad that you didn't decide to take an unscheduled trip to the Bahamas."

"Not my style," she dismissed curtly. "Tomorrow?"

"Eight o'clock."

She hung up, and David clapped his hands before shutting off his equipment. "That was great!" he told her. "You're a natural..." But he stopped short when he looked up to see her face. It was totally white. And as he watched, she swayed.

Leaping to his feet, he quickly jumped forward to catch and pull her against him. She didn't resist. In fact, her arms wrapped around him like he was her only life line on a violent sea.

"You okay?" he asked, folding her to his chest.

"Fine."

But she was shaking. He could feel her trembling from head to toe, and he couldn't blame her. The call had to have been unnerving, especially to someone with no experience in dealing with the lethal process of the criminal mind.

"Just give me a minute," she mumbled against his shoulder, and he hugged her gently in reassurance.

"Take your time," he told her and waited while her heart beat against his slowed to a more normal rhythm.

She shuddered. "I don't think I've ever been more scared. At least not since I went before Judge Lawson my first week out of law school."

"The Grizzly?" David asked, recognizing the name of the judge who was known for his bad temper and fierce scowl—not to mention his dislike for any attorney who wasn't totally prepared—or who wasn't in court on time when a case was called.

"The one and only," she agreed and pulled back slightly to look up at him. Her eyes were blue pools in a face that was still pale. "They really would have killed me."

He nodded at her soft whisper and lifted a gentle hand to brush the hair from her face. The innuendos and veiled threats had been warnings, and somebody would have carried them out if she hadn't been willing to cooperate and return the bag. "These type of people are usually sore losers."

She took a deep, steadying breath. "Thank you for being here."

"Happy to oblige," he grinned, but suddenly the temperature in the room was escalating and the source of the heat was his hands on her.

Through the silken robe she wore her flesh burned, the soft scent of her perfume tantalized, and with nothing but a couple pieces of material between his skin and hers, he abruptly realized he'd been right. Her suits did hide some interesting mounds and curves.

Yet even as recognition flashed in her eyes, even as his blood started to stir, he remembered why he was with her. Not to seduce but to protect. He didn't want, and wasn't about, to take advantage of the situation. Of her.

She was feeling vulnerable and scared, and if she looked good enough to eat, her response to him wasn't out of desire. She was reacting to what was happening. The stimulation was being provided by the situation not him.

Still, releasing her took more effort than he cared to admit, especially when, taking a step back and away from her, she swayed again. Toward him.

"I recorded the call," he announced sharply and reached for his equipment instead of her. But he was swearing—silently—at the race of excited pheromones that had heat pooling in his groin. "When we replay it, we might get some clues on the caller, and I have some friends who have access to voice pattern equipment. We could get lucky and find a match."

"Do you think so?"

The tremor in her voice made his fists clench as he straightened from the machine that now held potential evidence. "I know so."

She nodded understanding, but she didn't move. She remained where she was with her arms crossed in front of her, hugging herself against the chill that came from brushing up against the cold forces of greed and evil. He had to shove his hands in his pockets to stop himself from stepping forward to try to warm her up.

"You better get some rest." His voice seemed overly loud even to himself, but she didn't seem to notice. She simply shuddered.

"I don't think I can sleep any more."

"Try," he urged lowly, and he needed her to. For his sake and hers. He wanted her ready for the morning rendezvous, and her absence was the only way he was going to regain some peace of mind—and control over his rebelling body that was ready and willing to respond to hers.

"All right."

Her retreat was slow and uncertain, and he watched her go, holding his breath until she disappeared. When she vanished into the dark recesses of the hallway beyond and he heard a door softly shut, he collapsed onto the couch with a heartfelt sigh and abruptly found himself staring into the unblinking amber eyes of her cat. "What?" he asked the sleek animal. "You think I should have given her another hug?"

The cat continued to stare.

"Believe me, the comfort I would have offered would have involved a lot more than holding her hand," David muttered and watched the noble Arthur lift a front paw to begin the elaborate process of feline grooming. David groaned and drew a hand down over his face. "You've definitely slipped over the edge, Maverick. Now you're talking to cats."

His gaze drifted towards the shadows in the hall. Better her cat than her.

He blew out a troubled breath. Christine Dunn was a delicious morsel better left unsampled. He'd always suspected as much. She might have a tough front, but underneath the shell, she was soft. And vulnerable. She had hidden hurts and insecurities. Just like he did.

Abruptly turning his back to the rooms beyond the darkness, he rewound the tape in preparation of listening to it again. The process would provide a distraction, and he needed one. From his own personal demons and from desires better left unacknowledged and ignored.

He was a loner after all. It was how he liked it, how it had to be. His was a life filled with risk and uncertainty. One relationship had already been sacrificed to his need to be part of the machine that enforced justice, and his body bore the scars that testified to the danger he regularly encountered.

When next someone came at him with a weapon, he might not survive the attack. Or, worse, the next time he could end up blind. And he wasn't going to saddle anyone with his handicap.

Forcing himself to concentrate on the recording, he listened beyond the words for background noises or other giveaways and shut thoughts of Christine out of his mind. She didn't belong in his head. She didn't belong in his life except on the edge, and once the briefcase was delivered in a few hours, that's where she would be placed once more.

She would return to the safe world of legal phrases and courtroom melodrama, and he would be on his own again, chasing the bad guys. That was the way it should be. The way it had and the way he wanted it to remain. Or at least that's what he assured himself.

If he let her stick him back into the slot she'd assigned him to, he couldn't touch her, and she couldn't touch him. And that was best. For both of them. He was almost certain of it.

CHRISTINE GOT out of bed at six the next morning. Not that she'd been sleeping. She hadn't. Not since the phone call at three a.m., not since David had held her in his arms, and not since she'd clung to him in wanton abandon.

Yanking open the closet door, she stared unseeing at what hung inside. It would have been easy for him to take advantage of the situation, to use her fears as a way to keep her in his arms and get into her bed, but he hadn't. He'd let her go, and she was sorry.

Scowling at her own lack of control, she grabbed an eggshell blue suit from the rack along with a matching pastel blouse and headed for the dresser across the room. She needed to collect some more intimate under apparel before creeping out the door and into the bathroom.

Bumping a drawer open, she muttered to herself. She wasn't ready to meet him again. Not yet. And chances were good she wouldn't have to immediately. No sounds had come from beyond her bedroom door for at least two hours. Hopefully, that meant he was asleep, and she had time to prepare herself and to get into something less revealing than a flimsy nightgown and robe ...

Face flaming, she stepped into the shower short minutes later to turn the spray on full blast, but it didn't wash the heat from her cheeks or the memory of his body pressing against hers from her mind. That image was too vivid to be forgotten so quickly or easily. Still it wasn't one she was willing to repeat. She couldn't. She couldn't give into the attraction sizzling between them—even if he was much more appealing than she could ever have imagined.

The vulnerability of his nightmare might have shown her a whole other side to the man who was her business partner and associate, but that didn't and couldn't change who and what they were. Two people from totally different backgrounds with totally different goals.

Shutting off the water, she grabbed a towel to dry off with and frowned in concentration. Okay, their goals weren't *totally* different. They both, as he put it, wanted to get the "bad guys," but beyond that, their lifestyles didn't mesh. Or at least she didn't think they did.

Sighing, she attacked her hair and makeup with obstinate calm. The trouble was she really didn't know that much about David Maverick. She'd assumed a lot. Like his womanizing, for example, but the night before had proven her wrong.

With his dark good looks and the way the female clientele were always flirting with him, she figured when he wasn't on a professional case, he was on a personal one, but if he was that quick and easy with the ladies, why hadn't he ended up in bed with her last night?

It was the perfect stereotypical circumstance. The damsel in distress, the hero rushing to her rescue to give comfort—of the most intimate kind—in an effort to wipe away fear with need. And she would have let him if he'd tried.

The phone call had frightened, the undertones of suppressed violence in the conversation had unnerved, and David had been there to offer strength and compassion. But nothing more.

Fully dressed and ready to go, she stared at her reflection in the mirror over the sink. His lack of interest and follow through confused. Had she imagined the sparks of electricity snapping between them?

Her teeth worried her lower lip. She didn't think so. The subtle shifting of the ebbs and tides of active hormones always seemed to be humming between them. Just out of sight, they'd simply remained unacknowledged and ignored. Until a few hours earlier.

Yet opportunity hadn't brought fruition. Instead of accepting what she'd suddenly been willing to give, he'd set her aside, turned away, and she should be grateful. She wasn't a virgin waiting for her knight in shining armor. She knew what men wanted, and she wasn't going to be putty in anyone's hands. Especially not his.

Leaving the bathroom, she lifted her chin in defiance of unwanted desire and injured pride. If David could resist the call of nature, so could she. After all, she wasn't interested in him personally. Not really. Where he was concerned, she wanted only to have access to his knowledge and professional expertise so they could catch whoever the briefcase belonged to. Nothing more. Nothing at all, or so she told the mutinous little voice of her subconscious screaming denial in her ear.

Ignoring it and braced for confrontation, prepared to meet him with cool control and determined to put to rest any ideas he might have about changing their relationship, she was disappointed when he wasn't in the living room—and abruptly terrified when she realized his equipment was gone.

Panic grabbed her by the throat. Surely he hadn't left her. He couldn't have. Wouldn't have. Would he?

Rushing toward the front door, her thoughts ran into one another. Had he slipped out during the night? Left her alone with the briefcase? She couldn't believe it! Or could she?

Her heart lodged in her throat, and her footsteps faltered. What if the briefcase was what he'd been after all along? All that cash, all that talk of temptation. Had his purpose in joining her for the evening only been to grab the opportunity to take the money and run?

Gulping for air, she flew around the corner and into the dining room and stopped. The briefcase, along with another fatter bag, was sitting on the dining room table.

Stopping to touch both with trembling hands, she sucked oxygen into her lungs, willed her heart back into her chest and let her eyes drift toward the kitchen. It was the only room he might be in, and moving to the door, her pulse jumped when she stepped through the door and found him standing by the stove.

No longer naked from the waist up, the hard width of his chest was covered once more by shirt and suit coat, but if she'd thought he'd looked like a pirate in the dark, he looked more so in the breaking dawn with the stubble of a beard darkening his jaw. And suddenly he was looking at her, turning to pin her with a gaze that was dark and brooding but unexpectedly lightened when it fell on her.

"Care for a cup?" he asked, holding up a ceramic mug of coffee he had obviously just brewed.

Uncertain whether she should be relieved caffeine was so readily in reach and available or annoyed he was making himself at home in her house, she arched an eyebrow at him. "Found everything okay, did you?"

He grinned at her rebuke for his invasion of her personal space and watched her retrieve a cup from the cupboard. "Knowing you like coffee almost as much as I do, the least I could do after your hospitality is prepare a pot of sludge for you."

She took a sip and gasped. Sludge was an apt description of the thick, black liquid scalding her throat.

"Too rich?" he asked, his lips curving around his mug.

"It'll keep me awake." Probably for the next forty-eight hours, but she took another sip anyway. It gave her something to do while he was watching her. "Would you like something to eat?"

He shook his head and, draining his cup, set it down on the counter. "No, I've got to be going."

Her stomach flipped, and she hastily set her own cup aside to hide the sudden quake of her hand. "You're leaving me alone?"

"Can't stand to be without me already?"

Crossing her arms in front of her in an instinctive gesture of self defense, she met his satisfied smirk with a glare. "I could get used to being without you."

He winced. "Counselor, remind me never to be on the opposing side of you in court. You know just where to hit."

"Thank you."

"You're welcome. I think."

She glanced at the clock on the wall. "It's not even seven o'clock."

"And your meeting isn't until eight, I know, but I've got to get ready," he told her, shoving his hands in his pockets in a casual stance.

She frowned. "What are you going to do?"

"Get in position to take some photos, to get an overall view of the scene and get ready to follow whoever makes off with the case when it happens."

Her jaw dropped. "You're going after ..."

"How else am I going to find out where the case is taken?"

"But," she sputtered. "I thought ..."

"What? That you'd get to come along for the chase?"

Her eyes narrowed on him. "I'm the one who found the briefcase."

"You're also the attorney. I'm the private eye," he reminded her quietly. "You sit behind a desk or argue in front of judges. I sneak around finding and following people. It's my job."

She knew he was right. She just didn't like it. He was taking over and leaving her behind. Typical male behavior. She should have expected it. Him taking control.

"Chris, once you make the drop, you're out of danger," he continued logically. "And you're out of the picture. There's nothing more you can do."

She nodded, understanding coming on a wave of distaste. He'd obviously had it planned all along. "You used me."

He shook his head in denial of her accusation. "And you're going to use me to get to the truth."

She wasn't convinced. He'd set her up. From the start. He'd known as soon as the arrangements for the exchange were made, he wouldn't need her any more, and the case would be his. Yet he didn't back down under her glare. He stepped closer instead.

"I couldn't do this without you," he insisted. "I couldn't catch the bad guys or even try to find out who they are without your help."

"And when you discover who they are?"

He shrugged. "I don't know. Finding out where the briefcase is delivered can only be the first step. Once we figure out the who, then we'll need to figure out the why."

"We?"

"As soon as I find out where the bag ends up, I'll meet you back in the office. We're going to have to work together to decide what we should do next."

Surprise made her blink. "Promise?"

"We're a team. This is our case, not mine. As soon as I can be back in the office, I will be," he assured her. "Besides, I'm only one man. Even if I figure out who's running a racket in the courthouse, I wouldn't be able to do anything about it by myself—and neither will we as a pair."

"The police?" she suggested.

"Or the feds," he agreed. "I don't have the slightest idea of what we're getting into."

"As long as we can get out again."

His grin flashed. "Trust me."

She did. She just didn't trust the way her heart was pounding when he slipped out the door minutes later. She was the one who was walking into danger. She was the one about to meet some criminal on a street corner, but it wasn't herself she was worried about. It was him.

AT EIGHT IN the morning, the streets of downtown Los Angeles were thriving with life. Cars and trucks rumbled down the roads, men and women jammed the walks, and the hustle and bustle of another work day had people rushing to get to their offices on time.

It was an independent race that pitted each person against themselves. Everyone was on their own mission to punch or beat the clock and, absorbed in the hurry to please waiting bosses, no one paid much attention to those they passed on the way to their destination. No one, it seemed, except for Christine. Emerged in the depths of the pulse of the city, she was all too aware of everybody around her.

Pushing the sunglasses on her nose up to keep back the growing glare of day, the dark lenses also hid the nervous dart of her eyes as she tried to keep her gaze straight ahead instead of searching for someone else on the busy thoroughfare who was carrying a case just like hers.

Pausing to glance at her watch, she stepped aside as a young man in a dark suit sprinted for the door of a skyscraper—and abruptly had to dodge again when another on roller blades flew past on his quest to reach the end of the block.

She smothered a sigh. Los Angeles was anything but dull. The executives on the walks with her weren't all wearing traditional garb of suit and tie. Many were in jeans. And not everybody was in a hurry to get to where they were going. Time was critical for some but not all. Yet, for her, it was essential.

Keeping track of minutes was part of her life. Hearing dates and court appearances were set by schedule. Papers had to be filed within specified guidelines. Nothing in law could be done, it seemed, without worrying about the passing of a statute or time frame. Therefore, the clock was always on her mind, but never more so than it was at the moment.

Swallowing but finding little saliva in her mouth that was unnaturally dry, she eyed the corner not far ahead. She was a few minutes early. That meant she had to wait. Stall. And she took up a position by a building door and tried to act as if she were waiting for someone. Not that anyone noticed. Or at least nobody appeared to.

She was just another person on the busy sidewalk. At least to most. But someone nearby had to be watching her. Somebody besides David.

Calm came with knowing he was near. She wasn't really alone. She wasn't by herself. He was close. He was ready to come to her rescue if need be, if something went wrong, if she happened to turn at the wrong time and look the courier in the eye....

Fear coiled into a tight knot in her stomach, and she again raised her wrist to look at her watch.

What would happen if the anonymity she sought was lost? What if she accidentally met and recognized whoever was about to exchange luggage with her? Would she be shot on the spot or killed later? What on earth had she gotten herself into?

The people after the money were playing for keeps. To them this wasn't a game but business. Deadly business. And if she got in their way, she would be eliminated.

Finding it impossible to swallow again, the minute hands on her watch said it was time. She had to go, and stepping forward, she merged with the crowd surging toward the intersection and the stop light.

Immediately she felt lost. Swamped by the humanity around her. Squeezed from all sides, shoulders bumped hers, and she was carried forward on a hustling wave. Cresting, it abruptly peaked—and crashed—without warning when the "Don't Walk" sign lit and the traffic signal turned from green to yellow.

Trapped as people closed in to surround her, she came to a halt, and across the street, in plain view, David held his breath.

Was she going to freeze? Was she going to forget the prearranged sign of surrender? What if she didn't put the case down?

She was nervous. It showed in her body language, and he didn't blame her. She had good cause to be afraid, but nothing would happen—not to her—if she did what she was supposed to. But would fear stop her from fulfilling her role?

Suddenly, she moved. Juggling her purse, fussing with the case, she unexpectedly set the attaché on the cement and lifted a hand to brush her hair.

Air left his lungs on a sigh of relief. That was it! She'd given the signal, but that didn't mean the wait was over. His gaze narrowed on the throng around her, and silently he swore.

A million briefcases were in the crowd. Lawyers going to the courthouse a block away, businessmen going to a meeting, people carrying bags with their lunches and who-knew-what-else. It was nearly impossible to see. Christine was encircled by those who were taller or wider than she, but someone was moving within the log jam of bodies.

The flash of leg, the swing of an arm, the setting down of a case on the sidewalk next to hers. His heart thudded against his chest. It was happening. The switch. But a face eluded him. He had only a sleeve of a business suit, and before he could discern more, the race began again.

Traffic slowed, the light turned from red to green, and somebody in front stepped off the curb.

People surged forward, and he saw Christine swiftly bend to retrieve a case. She had to grope to find a handle, she had to keep her gaze locked ahead during the search, but she did it. And in seconds she was free. Marching with the crowd, she strode across the pavement and away from subterfuge and danger. Or so David thought—until the courier went after her.

Unexpectedly the man who'd switched cases at the intersection followed her steps, and David's stomach clenched in silent alarm. Yet he maintained his calm. And his cover.

Keeping the video camera he was using carefully aimed from where it was propped on his shoulder disguised within a "boom box," he strode forward. He had to stay with Christine and the courier.

Taking a parallel course from the other side of the road, he followed, determined not to let them out of his sight, but no one tried to sway him or get in his way. Quite the contrary, everybody gave him a wide berth. And he wasn't surprised.

Dressed in ratty jeans and a disreputable tee shirt, with a radio roaring in his ears and with no apparent destination, he was an oddity to be avoided and another screwball in the City of Angels to be ignored. And that served his purpose. By being too obvious, he was easy to overlook, but when the pursuit continued through another stop light, he was ready to cast disguise and the video aside to save her.

Yet suddenly rescue wasn't necessary. His interference wasn't needed. The man in the suit, the one on her tail, abruptly shifted course.

Away from Christine, the courier swerved right when she turned left to head for the office a few blocks away and in so doing, the man succeeded in keeping his back to the camera.

Clenching his teeth in frustration, David stayed with the briefcase and the person carrying it, keeping the video running and the boom box blaring as the courier changed direction again.

Taking David by surprise, the trail chosen didn't wind down the sidewalk and away toward a car that would force pursuit in the taxi stationed at the end of the block. The attaché was carried up the steps instead. Toward the courthouse doors.

Crossing the street to follow with an air of arrogant nonchalance, David continued with the foot traffic and traced his quarry's steps towards the halls of justice. But even as he prepared to continue the chase into the building, figuring the courier would go in one door only to immediately go out another once inside, the man carrying the attaché stopped.

Pausing, he turned his head back toward the street and David and after the retreating figure of Christine. The action gave David a clear view of the face inside the suit, and disbelief at the revealed identity took his breath away.

He knew the man. Knew him well. Respected him, too. Or he had.

The courier swung away and disappeared inside the courthouse, but David didn't bother to follow. There was no need. He knew where the man was going. Too well.

Releasing the button powering the video, he went past the stairs and continued on away from the building. His mission was over. What he'd wanted to accomplish was done. He could return to the office. All's he had to do was circle the block to do what he'd promised Christine he would. Get back to her as soon as possible.

Yet, swearing under his breath, he knew he was going to surprise her with the speed of his arrival. She wasn't going to be expecting his search to end so soon—any more than she would be anticipating the news he was going to bring her—and it was worse than either one of them could have possibly expected.

Chapter 5

CHRISTINE BURST into the office and nearly ran Mandy over. The only reason she could tell it was Mandy was the hairstyle. Of the twins, Mandy was the one who preferred wearing her shoulder length blonde hair in a braid.

"Are you okay?" Mandy asked, catching Christine's arm in alarm, and Christine knew why.

She was breathing like a freight train. Why she didn't know. She hadn't run far. Just from the elevator to the office door, but her heart was pounding a mile a minute. "Of course, why?"

Mandy glanced from her to the hallway that was disappearing behind the closing door. "You sound and look as if you were running from someone."

"Just in a hurry, that's all," Christine denied cheerfully, too cheerfully from the doubtful look on Mandy's face. "I'll just be in my office."

Mandy nodded, a frown darkening hazel eyes that were identical to her sister's.

"Where's Candy?" Christine asked, trying to divert her secretary's attention.

"It's Thursday," Mandy replied in way of explanation and made Christine's mind whirl.

"Thursday," Christine repeated, trying to remember how the car pool ran. Mandy had Tuesday, Candy had Thursday, the neighbors had Monday and Wednesday, and Friday was a rotation day where all four mothers took turns getting the kids to school. "The children?"

Mandy smiled. "You're getting better."

"Right," Christine agreed and dodged into her office and shut herself inside. She was never going to be able to keep her secretaries straight. It was bad enough she had trouble telling one from the other at times much less recall who was where when, but the debate of asking the twins to wear name tags and post a schedule was lost in the turmoil of the moment and in the dread of opening up her briefcase.

Walking to her desk, she set the attaché down and made great ceremony of putting away her purse in a drawer. What would she find inside? Just what she'd left? Or would there be something more?

Sitting in her chair, she studied the case while her teeth worried her lower lip. She wanted to delay the inevitable, perhaps wait for David, but thinking of him only spurred her to action. She didn't need a man present when she faced her demons. Besides curiosity was stronger than she was—and impossible to resist. She had to see what was inside.

Abruptly leaning forward to set the case on its side, she unsnapped the locks, held her breath and flipped the lid open.

Paper dazzled her eyes. Lots of it and in all forms. Folders, writing tablets, with the printed word and without. And there were pencils. Pencils and pens. All of which she'd put into the case herself a day earlier.

Collapsing into her chair, she stared. Everything appeared just as she'd left it. All that she had put inside still seemed to be there. Untouched, undisturbed and unmoved.

It was difficult to tell anyone had even looked through the pages. A chill shivered down her spine. But someone had. The man she'd talked to. The one who had subtly threatened her life.

Her mouth thinned, and she lifted the top folder. If something, some clue was inside, she was going to find it. And use it to find him.

One at a time, she pulled out and looked over and through each manila folder, flipped through the blank legal pads she always kept with her to make notes on and examined every piece of loose paper, but when she got to the bottom, the pile on her desk gave no indication whatsoever as to where the attaché had been, or with whom, overnight.

Slumping back in her chair, she glared at the silent leather case. The man hadn't left a clue. Not a smudge of evidence. Except for maybe a thumb print that she couldn't see.

She sighed. But even that seemed unlikely. Whoever her caller had been, he was a pro. She just hoped David was having more luck in digging up answers. And she hoped David was all right.

Remembering standing on the street corner, recalling the crush of people, the anxiety of uncertainty, the possibility of death and discovery, she couldn't imagine how or why anyone would want to be a private investigator. The surge of adrenaline, the loss of control, the sense of anticipation when it was happening and the exhilaration when it was all over....

She shook her head in disbelief. It had been terrifying—and exciting. The sense of adventure, danger, daring do, it was stimulating beyond imagination. The experience gave her insight into emergency room doctors who were adrenaline junkies and into David who, while enjoying the thrill, was also risking his life to follow a stranger into the unknown.

She looked to the door, wondering when he'd return and fearing he was walking straight into a trap.

If something happened to him, she didn't know what she'd do, but suddenly she knew how she'd feel. Lost. Alone. She would miss him. It amazed her to realize how much.

His smile, his daily attempts at light-hearted flirtation, his confidence and strength. Without even being aware, she'd become reliant on his presence. On him.

Regret washed through her. She should have taken the time to get to know him better, to understand him instead of wasting time assuring herself that he was just another typical male. He'd proven otherwise. Especially the night before.

He could laugh at himself, he could be strong, but he could also be vulnerable....

Voices abruptly filtered through her scattered thoughts. Mandy's and...David's!

Leaping from her chair, Christine raced to the door, threw it open and nearly cried with relief when she saw him. She managed to beam at him instead. "You're back!"

And he was. In a disgusting black tee shirt with a human skull emblazoned on it and in jeans with a hole in one knee and a tear in intriguing proximity to his well formed derriere, he was standing in the office still unshaven and scruffy looking but very much alive and safe. And soon!

Suddenly aware of Mandy gaping at her in stunned silence, Christine swallowed her joy at his safe return and hastily tried to correct her blurted greeting with a cool clarification. "I didn't expect you until later."

The attempt at decorum didn't work. Mandy's gaze slid from she to David and back again with obvious and growing speculation.

Gritting her teeth, wishing David had asked her for the address to her condo rather than one of the twins the day before, Christine knew trouble was brewing in the imagination department but couldn't spend time worrying about it at the moment. Not when she wanted to talk to him so badly. "Why don't you come into my office?" she suggested as calmly as possible. "We have so much to discuss."

"Yes, we do," he returned gravely, making her wince and Mandy's eyes widen even more.

But rumor and innuendo were a lot easier to deal with than her impatience, and when he got close enough, Christine grabbed his arm and dragged him into the room before nearly slamming the door. "What happened?"

"Not much," he denied, and she nearly hissed with frustration.

"What do you mean 'not much'? Did you see who took the briefcase? And how did you get back here so fast?"

"Our courier didn't go far," was his flat reply, and the light from the window in her office distracted her when she caught the glint of gold in his hair.

She stared. "Is that an earring?"

He lifted a hand to touch the ring caught in the lobe of his right ear. "Nice effect, don't you think?"

A patch, an earring. All's he needed was a kerchief for his head and a sword in his belt to complete the image of marauding pirate. She put her fists on her hips. "I want to know what happened."

"So do I," he agreed cryptically and reached for the doorknob. "Come to my office. I'll show you the tape."

"Tape? What tape?"

But he was already leaving, and she had to follow, well aware of Mandy watching their progress as they moved from one room to another in conspiratorial silence.

She closed the door behind him and waited impatiently as he set a huge boom box down on his desk. His office was the same size as hers, but the furniture in his was different. He had a desk and a filing cabinet like she did, but he also had a wardrobe-like cabinet he kept locked and a large stand that held a television set and a video machine. As she watched, he moved to the latter to slip a disk inside.

"Why don't you just tell me what happened?" she asked, aggravated by the delay.

"Because it's easier to show you," he said, hitting a button and stepping back with remote control in hand.

Forced to silence, she stared at the television screen until the street she'd been on a short time before came into view.

"This is you approaching the rendezvous site," he announced, and she spotted herself in the crowd, not an easy task considering how many people were on the walk.

"I was early," she murmured, and he grunted as her image on the screen halted by the door of a building and lifted an arm to look at the watch strapped to her wrist.

"I couldn't spot anybody with an identical briefcase," he told her. "I didn't even see the courier until he was in the crowd behind you."

She scowled at all of the people holding one type of attaché or another as her image finally began moving toward the corner. "Too many lawyers."

"I know a lot of people who'd agree with you."

She glanced from the television to glare at him but hastily looked back again to watch the crowd close in around her at the curb. There were a lot of bodies, a lot of legs and arms and action, and she almost missed it when the attaché was set down next to hers. "There!"

"Yes," he agreed, squinting at the screen. "But I didn't get a good look at him until later."

She chewed at her lip as she waited to see what he already had, for her image to cross the street and the man in the suit to turn and walk the other way, and she held her breath when the courier went toward the door, paused on the steps—and looked straight into the camera. She gasped. "It can't be!"

"It is," David confirmed grimly. "Somebody I'd never suspect."

"But...are you sure you followed the right man?"

"See anyone else in the crowd with the same briefcase? See anyone else looking after you?" he demanded, obviously as unhappy with his discovery as she was.

"I can't believe it," she whispered and moved closer to the television to watch the man disappear through the courthouse doors.

"Believe it," David snapped. "Our courier is none other than The Honorable Curtis C. Wilson, Judge and duly elected public official."

"You sound bitter," Christine said, turning to stare at David in dismay.

"I am," he agreed, his mouth a thin, angry line. "The police trust him. Every officer I know sees him as 'Justice's Judge.' He's tough on crime and criminals. He helps cops put felons behind bars, and now it turns out he's a felon himself."

"You don't know that!" she objected.

David snorted and gestured to the television. "Want me to run the tape again?"

"There has to be another explanation," she denied and earned a scowl.

"Why are you so eager to defend him?"

"Because he was my teacher, because he is my friend and because I can't believe he'd do anything like this."

"The evidence is clear, counselor," David denied and yanked the earring off to throw it on his desk.

"I'm going to go ask him."

She was moving toward the door before he could stop her. She had it open before he could grab her, but he slammed it in her face before she could step outside. "Just where the hell do you think you're going?"

"To confront him," she snapped, trying to shake David's hand off her arm.

"Just like that?" he demanded. "You're going to march into his chambers and ask him what he was doing picking up a briefcase filled with money?"

"Why not?"

"And how are you going to answer his question?" David asked. "What are you going to say when he wants to know what you were doing with it in the first place?"

"I'll tell him the truth."

"And he'll believe you?"

"Why wouldn't he?" she argued. "Besides, you're my witness, and you have the tape."

"Yes," David agreed. "*I* do."

She hissed and crossed her arms over her breasts to glare at him. "Meaning?"

"We go together."

"He doesn't know you," she protested when David turned to walk away toward the washroom tucked in the corner of his office. "He knows me."

"That's supposed to make a difference?" he asked, abruptly grabbing the hem of the tee shirt and stripping it off to toss it into a nearby chair.

She gulped at the sudden display of sinew and muscle and against the shaft of heat that shot through her. Abruptly she remembered how his skin had felt under her palms the night before, how hot his flesh was, how smooth, and the only way she could continue the argument was by quickly looking away as he stalked inside the room to yank open the small cabinet above the sink. "He trusts me."

"After he saw you handling dirty goods?"

"It wasn't my fault!" she shot back, striding to the door to watch him smear shaving lotion across his jaw. "He'll understand."

David grunted, and she retreated. There was something intimate in watching a man shave, especially when he was half naked and standing in a bathroom.

"There has to be an explanation," she insisted and was greeted by a long stretch of silence before he finally spoke again.

"You sound sure of yourself."

"I'm sure of him," she denied and swung back to see David standing in the door, half his face clean shaven, the other half buried in white foam. She lifted her chin in defiance. "He's a good man."

David sighed. "I always thought so."

"We can't jump to conclusions."

"Every man is innocent until proven guilty?"

She nodded. "That's the law."

He reluctantly sighed agreement. "All right. Why don't you have Mandy call Wilson's chambers to see when his court's in session and when we've got a chance to see him?"

Victory nearly made her smile, but any joy was swiftly and unexpectedly swept away by the assault of sudden doubts. "Do you think it's safe to go there?"

David met her gaze but said nothing as she shook her head at her own impulsive reaction that would have seen her charge in to confront and demand.

"What if he's being watched?"

"What if *you* are?" David asked.

Fear curled around her throat. "Am I?"

"I don't know. Not for sure. Both of you belong in the courthouse, and you said the two of you are friends."

"We are," she agreed quietly. Her head dropped. "Or we used to be."

He came to stand before her, his hand settling gently on her arm. "Let's go find out if you still are."

Her eyes lifted and locked with his. She saw the sympathy, the understanding and abruptly felt the static. Snapping from her to him and back again, its spark ignited a flash of heat that robbed her of breath, of will and made her knees knock when his gaze focused on her mouth.

Shocked to silence, she could almost taste his lips, feel the pressure of his body straining against hers. His angles to her curves. And as she watched, his head dipped—and he suddenly jerked back.

"Have Mandy make that call." It was an order, a harsh demand, and he made it before spinning away to return to the sink and his razor.

His retreat made her grab the doorknob for support. Her legs felt like water, her blood like liquid mercury bubbling under the hot sun, and her lungs wouldn't work. Still she did what he asked. Somehow, she got out the door, mumbled a request to a curious Mandy and retreated into her office to hide in silence and reflect.

She hadn't imagined the heat the night before. And if David hadn't followed or led her into bed, it wasn't because he wasn't interested. He just wasn't giving in to any pagan urges. Even if, unbelievably, she wanted him to.

"I'LL DO THE talking."

David rolled his eyes as Christine moved up the stairwell in front of him. They were on their way to meet Judge Wilson, to confront a man who was possibly laundering money for who knew who, and she was still determined to be in charge. And he was still having trouble keeping his mind on his work.

He stifled a groan as her backside swished back and forth in front of him as she climbed each step.

A private investigator, a former cop, he was used to digging for clues and ferreting out information. He was good at reading people and understanding their motives, but he was at a loss to explain where the explosion of heat between he and her had come from.

They'd worked with each other for months. Aware of one another, they'd kept their distance and remained professional partners, but one night on her couch and he was ready to drag her off somewhere to make mad and passionate love to her until he could no longer stand and she couldn't move.

Why the sudden attraction? Or, perhaps the question was, why now? It wasn't as if he hadn't recognized the sizzle of chemistry between them before. He'd simply ignored it because it was what she'd wanted. The trouble was, she didn't seem to want it any more, and he wasn't sure that was a good thing.

They weren't exactly made for each other. Not only was she not his type, he didn't think he was hers either. Solid, dependable, boring. He nearly grimaced. Solid, he didn't think he was. Dependable, maybe. Boring, he sure the hell hoped not. He shook his head. It didn't matter. The bottom line was simple. He wouldn't be good for her, or she for him.

A liaison between them would not only be unwise, it would be unfortunate because she wouldn't see it as a one-night stand. The two of them couldn't join only to relieve physical needs and enjoy a few hours. Any rendezvous, for her at least, would be the first step towards happily ever after, and he just wasn't a happily-ever-after type of guy. Not any more than he was close to being Price Charming. He had the scars to prove it.

"You won't mind if I say a word or two?" he asked, smiling when she glared at him over her shoulder.

"Just don't upset him," she ordered, pausing to wait for him to stop beside her when they reached the landing and the hall leading to Wilson's office and chambers.

"Why would I want to do that?" David asked as she began moving with him again. "Just because the man's helping someone transport gobs of money without reporting it to the IRS, I wouldn't want to ask him any questions that he wouldn't like to answer."

"That's not funny."

"It wasn't supposed to be," he countered as they walked and didn't blink when she turned to confront him.

"You said you'd give him a chance."

"I will," David agreed. "I'm very interested in what he has to say."

Her eyes narrowed on him.

"I'll follow your lead," he offered and held out a hand to gesture in the direction they had to go. But if he was suggesting peace, he was ready to make war. He wasn't going to leave Wilson's chambers without finding out what he wanted to know, and he wasn't above blackmail to get what he wanted.

It was likely Wilson would try to throw them out when the first question came. David figured the video he had of the briefcase exchange would be enough to stop the ousting. The tape wasn't evidence enough to prove anything, but it was enough to start an investigation. And, unless he missed his guess, the judge wouldn't want that to happen. Still David hoped it wouldn't be necessary.

Like Christine, he wanted to give the man the benefit of the doubt. Wilson had done too many good things for the city's law enforcement to not give him an opportunity to defend himself. David just didn't know if any defense would be good enough to justify whatever the judge was hiding.

"Christine, what a pleasant surprise!"

Following her through the door emblazoned with Wilson's name, David watched a woman he guessed to be pushing fifty turn from a computer terminal to smile at both of them. She wore half moon glasses, a dress and blazer that were both navy blue and professionally cut, and she had hair that kept gray at bay with a bottle.

"I was hoping to catch him in," Christine suggested, stopping before the woman's desk that was littered with paper, folders of varying sizes and a calendar reflecting the day's schedule.

"If he has a minute, Ms. Baker," David agreed, reading the name plate on the desk and nodding amiably to Wilson's secretary.

Arlene Baker shook her head. "The judge always has time for Christine. Not that he has any favorites."

Her wink was friendly and encouraging as she silently waved them toward the door at the side of the room, but Christine didn't move right away. David's hand in the small of her back was needed as a prompt. His touch also helped steady nerves he could tell were taut by the way she was clutching her briefcase.

"Relax," he murmured in her ear and reached around her for the knob. "I'm right behind you."

Her answering nod was jerky and her smile forced. The coming meeting wasn't one she was looking forward to. Dread clearly reflected on her face.

"Deep breaths," he encouraged, wondering at the closeness between judge and attorney, but those questions would come later. He pushed the door open, and she led the way inside.

The room, when entered, was bright and airy. Lit by sunshine from the windows and fluorescent bulbs in the ceiling, no shadows hid the bookcases jammed with volumes containing legal phrases, case citings and California statutes, and the desk was buried, too.

Huge oak, its surface was covered with "in" and "out" boxes that were both overflowing and by a mass of folders that was intimidating at best and daunting at worst. Even the chairs were ladened with the debris of decision making, of ministering justice and of insuring every accused was granted their equal and legal rights.

Yet one chair held more than the written word. It held a man. Once dark, his hair was thin and graying, and his face bore the lines of time and age. The eyes that lifted from the examination of the brief or motion didn't show the wear of years, though. Their dark depths held intelligence and authority and brightened noticeably when they settled on his visitors.

"Christine!"

She immediately stepped forward to be swept into a warm embrace, but if the meeting held joy for both of them, it also held pain.

Standing back, watching the interaction of two people he knew and respected, David focused on the judge. He saw happiness darken to disappointment, and it was an emotion mirrored in Christine's expression. The morning's events had seen these two hurt each other, but neither of them were willing to speak of it. Both were ready to pretend the pain didn't exist, but he was there to make sure they remembered it and more.

"You brought a friend," Wilson said, stepping back to gesture to David.

"David Maverick, Your Honor," he greeted, stepping forward to accept the firm hand clasp of a man his uniformed comrades had always admired.

"Maverick," Wilson repeated and looked to Christine, obviously not recognizing the name.

"My associate," Christine clarified and glanced at David, a silent plea for understanding in her eyes.

"An attorney?" Wilson asked David.

"No, a private investigator," he responded and watched the older man's gaze turn wary. "Christine and I share office space."

"Yes," she quickly agreed. "It helps to have someone with his talents around for those personal injury cases."

David remained silent, watching the interplay, observing the body language and feeling the tension in the room rise. Christine's nervousness was growing more apparent. Her motions as she stood awkwardly by the judge were jerky, and her smile was forced and uneasy.

Wilson recognized the symptoms and asked, "Your background?"

"I used to be a cop," David responded and lifted a hand to point to the patch covering his one eye. "Until a machete got in the way."

Wilson nodded understanding and glanced at Christine before retreating a step to put the desk in between them. "Unfortunate."

"Part of the job," David denied with a shrug. "And it has allowed me to stretch a bit, get into the detective mode without waiting for a promotion."

"Yes, I'm sure it has," Wilson agreed and smiled at Christine. "But as happy as I am to see you and meet Mr. Maverick, I'm afraid this case I'm working on needs some attention."

"And we don't want to keep you," David agreed before she could speak and earned a glare from her for his efforts, but he ignored her and centered on the judge. "We just wanted to ask you a question."

"Yes, we did," she agreed, her chin lifting at his challenging prompt. She wasn't going to let him carry the ball alone, and she wasn't going to allow him to make the accusation.

He watched her turn back to face the judge.

"I was at the courthouse yesterday," she told him. "It was rather difficult getting around."

Wilson grunted. "The Hollywood Harem case. We'll all be glad when it's over."

"I got caught in the hall," she hurried on. "I had to set my briefcase down."

Wilson went very still.

"When I got to the office and opened it..."

"She discovered a case full of money," David interrupted and watched Wilson frown.

"Someone had switched cases with you?" he asked. "You called the police, of course?"

"I convinced her not to," David denied and quietly moved closer to the desk. "I realized that if it was turned over to the police, it would end up in the property locker where it would sit indefinitely and where it couldn't be used to find out who it belonged to."

Wilson's expression gave nothing away, but David expected no less. The man had sat on the bench too long. He knew how to school his emotions. His occupation demanded his ability to hide personal prejudice.

"We set up a sting instead, used the briefcase as bait, and I think you know who we got on the hook—and on video tape."

"Why?" Christine abruptly blurted before the judge could react. "Why were you the one to pick up my briefcase?"

Wilson took a deep breath, to steady himself, or to keep himself silent, David couldn't be sure. But suddenly the man looked old. Older than his fifty some years, and if he remained erect in his seat, his shoulders slumped under an invisible weight.

"You have the exchange on video?"

David nodded, not looking away from Wilson's direct gaze or the shadows that had appeared behind it.

"Can I convince you not to use it?" Wilson asked. "To trust me?"

"That depends on what you're willing to tell me."

Wilson sighed defeat, and his face crumpled. "I can tell you, Mr. Maverick, that if you release that video, if you tell the police about the exchange, my son is going to die."

Chapter 6

CHRISTINE GASPED. "No!"

"Explain," David demanded.

"It's simple, Mr. Maverick," Wilson complied, sitting heavily in his chair. "I'm being blackmailed." He looked to Christine and smiled. "But at least I haven't lost you. I thought I had this morning."

Her answering smile trembled. "Me, too."

"I think we all were surprised by who showed up at the exchange," David interrupted, unwilling to let the conversation's topic be changed. "But that doesn't explain how or why it happened."

Wilson hesitated. "I can't convince you to walk away?"

David slowly shook his head, sharing a brief but unyielding glance with Christine who was wavering toward being lenient and leaving. "You're going to have to trust us with the truth."

"Very well, but understand that by trusting you, I'm also entrusting you with my son's life." Obviously uneasy, Wilson stood once more to pace to a window and back again. "The briefcase was a test. It was a way for me to prove I could be relied on to cooperate with a plan."

"That involves?" David prodded.

"A case I have on my docket. The defendant is a young man who was caught by the police with a trunk filled with drugs."

David frowned. "I think I read about it in the paper. He was peddling his wares to some children."

"Yes, and he was parked next to the school yard."

"He's blackmailing you?" Christine asked.

"No, not him. His father," Wilson denied. "You see, his father doesn't want to see his son go to jail, and he will. He *should* if the district attorney makes his case the way I believe he will."

"But?" David prompted.

"I'm supposed to find a way to dismiss the case."

Christine shook her head. "How, if the evidence is so clear?"

"By throwing the evidence out."

Her jaw dropped, and Wilson continued.

"When the defendant's attorney argues that the police conducted an illegal search, that they had no probable cause to detain the defendant and that the defendant was doing nothing to draw attention to himself or to make the arresting officers believe he was doing anything illegal, I'm supposed to agree."

"But if you throw the evidence out, without the drugs, a conviction will be impossible," Christine protested.

"Exactly," Wilson agreed. "And without a conviction, the young man who makes money peddling dope to kids will go free."

"And his father will be extremely happy," David agreed. "But how does that affect your son's life?"

"My son's been kidnapped."

Christine murmured in distress, but Wilson went on as if he hadn't heard her.

"He was at the house, visiting during Spring break from college. The case had already been put on my docket when he left to go back to school, but he never got there. When I rose the next morning, his car was back in my driveway."

"A ransom note?" David asked.

"On the driver's seat."

"You didn't call the police?"

"The note said if I did, my son would be killed." Wilson held up his hand before David could speak again. "I know what you're going to say. I never would have believed if I was ever in this situation that I wouldn't turn to the law enforcement community to help me, but my son's all I have left."

And he was. David knew it. Every cop in the city knew it because some of those in uniform had been there to watch when Wilson's wife and daughter were pulled from the wreckage that had been their car after someone had run a red light and killed them both.

Every department in Los Angeles County had sent a representative to the funeral, to pay honor and lend support to the man who always backed them when he sat on the bench, who tried not to allow lawyers to twist the law to their needs and who did his best to keep justice in the halls of the courthouse.

David remembered hearing about it, reading about it, seeing the procession on the evening news. Curtis Wilson was a well-known member of the community, politically active, not afraid to be heard. His time in the spotlight also made him a potential target. "You know that whether you work with them or not, your son might still die."

"I know."

The acknowledgement was filled with grief and helplessness, and Christine responded to it. "There has to be a way to stop them, to find

Jimmy."

"I haven't been able to think of one," Wilson said and sank again into his chair.

"What about recusing yourself from the trial, having another judge hear the case?" she suggested.

"If I try to excuse myself or attempt to have the case shifted to another court, they'll kill Jimmy," Wilson denied.

"You could let the jury decide the case instead of making a ruling on any objection regarding the seizure of evidence," she tried again.

"The defendant has requested a bench trial."

David watched her chew at her lip. A bench trial was conducted at the accused's prerogative. Instead of being tried by a jury of his peers, the person charged could choose to have their case pled to one person. The judge.

"What if the district attorney..."

"The district attorney isn't going to object to a bench trial," David interrupted, forcing her to look at him. "Why should he? He's got his favorite judge on the bench. The DA trusts Curtis Wilson."

"Yes," Wilson agreed, his shoulders bowing further under an unseen weight, but David knew how heavy the load was.

Blind siding the DA would also knock the feet out from under the police. It would cause doubt in every arresting officer and destroy the faith Wilson had built between the court and the cops on the street.

Christine paced back and forth, unwilling to give up. "There has to be a way."

"There might be if we had a name," David suggested. "Tell us who the father is."

Wilson hesitated.

"It'll be easy enough for me to find out if you don't tell us," David prompted, sympathetic but relentless in his quest. He could get the name of the arrestee from the court docket or from his friends at the L.A.P.D., but it would speed things up if Wilson cooperated.

Wilson looked from David to Christine. "Mark Sherman."

Air hissed through her teeth. "Sherman!" She slammed her briefcase onto the desk top, scattering papers. "An attorney! An officer of the court! I can't believe even he'd stoop so low as to blackmail a judge."

"It's his son who's going to jail if this case goes forward," Wilson shrugged. "And you know as well as I that not all attorneys are ethical."

"He hasn't been for years," David observed, familiar with the name but more familiar with the clientele Sherman represented. The riffraff of the streets. Thieves, con men, pushers. Sherman did his best to keep them all out from behind bars and was paid well for it. "But he's not high enough up on the food chain to have the kind of pull it takes to make a kidnapping happen."

"You wouldn't think so," Wilson agreed, frustration and impotent rage stiffening his jaw.

"But someone pays his bills," David speculated. "And whoever that is, by helping Sherman out, by making you, a judge, bend to their will, they figure to end up with a judge in their pocket."

Christine's jaw dropped. "Do you realize what you're saying?"

David nodded at Wilson. "They're planning on using this against you for the rest of your term on the bench. Whenever it suits their purpose, they'll remind you of your little transgression and threaten to expose you in order to make sure you rule their way."

The judge shook his head once. Decisively. "No, they won't. As soon as I have my son safely back, I'll resign."

"Then they still win," David objected lowly. "Whether they get you on their side or whether you resign, they get a judge who's tough on crime and criminals out of the way."

"I won't risk my son's life!" Wilson yelled, slamming his fist down on his desk.

"Maybe you won't have to," David told him. "Not if we can find him before the hearing date."

CHRISTINE'S EYES widened as she stared at David. "What are you suggesting?"

"That we find Jimmy Wilson before Mark Sherman's son comes to trial."

"But how?" Wilson demanded, hope lighting his eyes.

David shrugged noncommittally. "Tell me how this all happened first. After the ransom note, what came next?"

"The note said I'd be contacted," Wilson explained. "And I was. By Sherman. He came here to talk about it with me."

"Here?" Christine asked in disbelief. "He came here? In chambers to talk blackmail?"

Wilson pointed to the one other empty chair in the room sitting opposite his desk. "He sat right there and told me it was my son for his. That when he got his son out from behind bars, I'd get mine back as well."

She paced her way from one side of the desk to the other,

smothering outrage and fear. Sherman was the type of lawyer who gave those who practiced law a bad name. She'd known it for a long time, and like most attorneys she was familiar with, she avoided him even if she couldn't avoid the talk about him.

Still, Sherman had sunk to a level below which she thought even someone with his reputation could go. He was willing to compromise his ethics even more than he did already by threatening a judge for his own gain, a threat that could lead to the loss of another's life.

She looked to David, willing and wanting to believe he could help find a way to save that life and save the judge's career, too. "What can we do?"

"Start digging, quietly, subtly. I've got friends who can ask questions."

"But if Sherman finds out," Wilson started to object.

"He won't and neither will his employer," David assured him. "You'll have to trust me."

Wilson stared at him for a long moment. "I do." He looked to Christine. "And you already know I trust you."

She smiled, but David spoke before she could.

"What about the briefcase?"

Wilson reached down to drag it out from under his desk. "It's still here. I'm supposed to drop it off tonight on the way home."

"Where?"

"At a parking structure." The judge named an intersection a short drive from the courthouse.

"What time?"

"Six o'clock. I'm to drive to the top level and leave it in the back of a red pick up."

David nodded. "You won't be alone."

Wilson's mouth opened to argue against it.

"You won't see me," David assured him. "And neither will anyone else."

"I'll make sure they don't," Christine agreed, determined David wasn't going to leave her out of the chase this time, and he wanted to protest. She could see it in the golden brown of his gaze, but he swallowed it. At least for the moment. She turned back to the judge. "I'll do everything I can to help you."

"I know you will," Wilson acknowledged and reached out to squeeze her hand before looking to David. "You'll stay in touch?"

"I will," he agreed, and Christine liked the way he accepted the judge's firm hand clasp. With confidence and understanding. "You do the same."

She picked up her briefcase and sighed. "I guess there's just one more question. How much time do we have before the court date?"

Wilson glanced from her to David. "The hearing's next Wednesday."

Christine felt her stomach drop. It was Thursday. Thursday afternoon. The lump in her throat threatened to choke her. "A week. We have less than a week."

"Then we'll have to work fast," David suggested and stepped toward the door. "Let's get going."

Numb, she moved with him, smiling mindlessly to Arlene Baker before following him out into the hall. "Blackmail."

"It could have been worse," he told her, keeping his voice low as they passed others in the corridor.

"How?"

"He could be crooked, accepting bribes."

The comment reminded her of the briefcase. "What do you think the money is from?"

"Your guess is as good as mine," he told her, jogging with her down the steps to the first floor. "Drugs, gambling, guns. It doesn't really matter. What does is the 'test.' By making Judge Wilson pick up the briefcase and then drop it off, they're insuring he'll do what they want."

"Aid and abet the commission of a crime." She shook her head and hurried to keep up with his long strides as they once again stepped into the day's sunshine. "I wish we could go to the police."

"We may have to."

"But..."

"I said may," he clarified before she could finish any objection. "I want to have a look around first, see where the briefcase takes me..."

"Us."

"You're not coming with," he insisted, hustling her across a busy intersection and ignoring the flashing "Don't Walk" sign.

"Try to stop me," she responded and yanked free of his guiding touch when they hit the opposite corner.

He swung to face her grimly. "You're not coming."

"I know the time and address just as well as you do," she countered, going toe-to-toe with him, oblivious to the pedestrians flowing around them.

"It could be dangerous!" he sputtered hotly. "Besides, you don't know anything about tailing someone."

"So teach me."

"There's no time," he denied, adamantly chopping air with his hand for emphasis. "If you come along, you'll just get in the way."

Unmoved by his growl or his argument, she took a step backward. "Fine. If you won't let me come with you, I'll go by myself." She spun to leave, but he wasn't about to let her get away.

Reaching out, he grabbed and pulled her back. "Don't be ridiculous!"

"I can do what I want!" she snapped, ignoring the bite of his fingers as they curled over her upper arms.

"What you want could get you hurt—or worse!"

The shake he gave her had her teeth snapping together, but hauled up onto her toes, she wasn't about to give up. She was ready to fight. Tossing her head back, she prepared to demand her release but stuttered instead when her gaze slammed into his.

He was furious. Anger glittered in his glare. It also vibrated through him and into her. The strength of it took her breath away. And her words. Yet she wasn't the only one who abruptly couldn't talk. Speech apparently escaped him, too. Even if action didn't.

Without warning his head drove downwards, and his mouth locked over hers.

Stunned, she hung suspended.

Paralyzed, she absorbed the punishment he wanted to give.

Shocked, she wanted to resist and fight back. But she couldn't.

He overwhelmed her. Her curiosity did. About him.

Maybe she'd never admitted it to herself, but she'd wondered. The women who were his clients, the ladies who he spent time with. What would it be like to be one of them? To be held in his arms? To be consumed by his kiss?

She may have ignored his flirtations, she might have succeeded in keeping him at arm's length, but her imagination had responded to him even if she hadn't. And he seemed to understand.

Even as he tried to grind her lips against her teeth, even as he attempted to intimidate, to get her to back off and leave him alone, his embrace softened, his mouth eased its pressure, and damnation turned into exploration.

He was curious, too. About her, and the thought thrilled and terrified her.

He was just a man, but he was a man like no other she'd ever dreamed of being possessed by. David represented the bad boy, the rebel. He was the type of potential partner she always avoided. Her preference was for the more controlled and disciplined male. After all, if she got involved, she wanted it to be with someone she could depend on.

David wasn't dependable. Not for the long term. He was foot loose, and he was dangerous because of the way he clung to his freedom. He wasn't what or who she wanted, or needed. He wasn't her dream come true, but the flames he was fanning were melting her resistance.

They burned, scorched, threatened to consume, but he managed to evade them even if she couldn't.

Gradually he drew back and in so doing allowed her feet to return to solid cement, but he didn't speak. She didn't either. Together they simply stood and stared. At each other.

Around them other men and women walked and talked. Nearby cars rumbled along the street, but she wasn't aware of the people or the machines. She was only aware of him. Of his breathing. Hers. Both were ragged.

"I shouldn't have done that."

The whisper didn't sound like an apology, but she didn't want one. "Don't do it again." Her voice held little conviction and, silently, she was already hoping he would make another attempt.

He didn't, but he didn't move away either. He stayed close, not losing eye contact with her. "What if I can't help myself?"

Her heart skipped against her ribs. "Try. We're both adults."

"Don't remind me," he murmured.

She licked her lips and regretted it instantly. His gaze zeroed in on the motion, and her pulse rate accelerated to warp speed. Suddenly unsure of herself, of what to say, and desperate to find something to focus on besides him and the need he'd awakened, she tried to return his attention to the case. "What are we going to do between now and six o'clock?"

His grin was delicious. It sent chills of awareness down her spine and put intimate images in her head. Of him and her. Together. Hot sex in the afternoon.

A flush filled her cheeks, she stammered, and he sighed in regret.

"What I'm going do is go ask questions," he told her.

"Of who?"

An eyebrow arched in wry humor. "You don't have to know everything."

Willing to concede him a point, she nodded but was quick to qualify her acquiescence. "Just when and where am I supposed to meet you for the drop?"

He looked away, and she held her breath. He still didn't want her to go. A silent moment passed before he returned his gaze to her. "You're too stubborn for your own good."

"I prefer the word tenacious," she qualified hopefully. "Just ask Bill Zaworski."

David lifted a hand to brush the lingering bruise on her cheek. "I don't have to. I was there, remember?"

Unwilling to be distracted by his charm, she shook her head. "Don't lock me out on this, David. I want to help."

He hesitated. "You're very close to the judge."

She bit her lip and let her eyes drop momentarily from his. "In law school, he took me in. Me and some others. He invited us to his house at night to debate and argue. He encouraged us to think. He made us learn and appreciate the law, and he shared his home."

"You met his wife?"

She smiled. "Katherine. She was wonderful. Always cooking, teasing, listening to our fears and worries. And his daughter." She took a deep breath, remembering the loss and the cold wind that had been blowing the day both women had been put in the cold, hard ground. "We were the same age."

His hand closed over her arm again in silent understanding. "They were what you wanted your family to be."

She sighed, not denying his recognition of the truth. "They were what I always thought a family should be. They cared about each other. They shared, and nobody's opinion was ever more important than anyone else's."

"Unlike in yours."

"My father decided what was best for all of us. When we moved, when we stayed, what we wore, what we did and who we did it with," she agreed but shoved the past away with an impatient gesture, oddly relieved rather than ashamed at having laid herself bare to him. "The judge can't lose Jimmy. It would destroy him, and I can't let that happen. I have to do something."

Slowly, David nodded. "I'll be back in the office by four. Be ready."

Relieved, thankful, her smile trembled. "I will."

He let her go and took a step backwards. "And find something to wear that's more comfortable than what you've got on. We may end up walking. Or running."

Fear shuddered through her. He wasn't kidding. What they were doing could be dangerous. “I’ll be waiting.”

He shook his head before lifting and dragging a hand through his hair. “I must be crazy.”

“No,” she denied. “You just know better than to argue with a lawyer.”

“A pretty one.”

Her pulse skipped, and the wind blew, ruffling his dark hair above the black patch. He looked rakish. Like a pirate. Her pirate. One she would have to deal with because as he silently turned to disappear into the crowd, she knew they had unfinished business.

Suddenly conscious of the hum and hustle of people and traffic around her, she quickly swung from curious glances and annoyed stares and moved out of the way and into the stream of pedestrians moving up the block toward her office building. Yet it was difficult to concentrate on where she was going. She kept thinking about him.

It was an impossible situation. The two of them. He was everything she didn’t want in a man. Dark, good looking, reckless. He lived on the edge and enjoyed it. She liked the mundane and embraced it.

If she was looking for an emotional entanglement—and she wasn’t—he would be her last choice for a partner in passion, but the attraction between them was volatile. It sizzled constantly and, exposed, it was impossible to ignore. Or so it seemed.

Pushing her way into the building, her eyebrows drew together in a studious line. Just because they both had the itch didn’t mean they had to scratch it. As she’d told him, they were adults, and adults could reason and resist.

She and he had been together for months without any lusty outbursts. That wouldn’t have changed if she hadn’t picked up the briefcase, if the element of danger and suspense hadn’t come between them and heightened their awareness of each other—man to woman.

She stepped into the elevator, but the ride to the third floor was brief. Soon she was striding purposefully down the hall to the office door.

It was time to put things back in perspective. David was her co-worker. Nothing more. She didn’t want him to be anything else because anything personal that happened between them would be no more than a fling, the giving in to a momentary craving, and she didn’t need that type of disruption in her life.

Everything was finally falling into place. Her practice was growing, the bills were being paid on time, she had a home she liked and a sense of continuity, permanency, that she'd always wanted. A romp in the sack with David wouldn't enhance her success. It would only point out her failure.

Her steps slowed.

She was alone. By herself, and he reminded her of what it could be like to be with someone, to be part of a team. Her shoulders stiffened. It was better to be alone than under someone's thumb. Better to be on her own than living by the dictates of another, and he was already trying to tell her what to do—and what not to.

That wouldn't happen again. Not to her. She'd come too far, fought too hard to become independent and to take control of her own destiny. She wasn't going to give it away.

Shoving through the door, she was greeted by a chorus of hellos from the twins. The sound was reassuring, and their respect for her as a boss confidence building. She didn't need a man to make her life complete. Perhaps eventually she'd seek a mate, someone she could live and share and have children with, but she wasn't ready yet.

"Any messages?" she asked.

"A few," Mandy agreed, rising from her desk to hand her several pieces of paper. "And I've got that brief finished. If you want to breeze through it, I can get it down to the courthouse and filed today."

"Great," Christine smiled, continuing on to her door with Mandy trailing behind.

"Is David coming back?"

The question came from Candy and stopped Christine in mid-stride. Slowly she turned to glance from one twin to the other. Their expressions reflected total interest, and their eyes gleamed with unsupported speculation. "He'll be back around four. Why?"

"A report," Candy offered with not so much as a blink. "He wanted it done today and mailed, but he has to read it first."

Christine nodded, not convinced by the guileless hazel gazes fixed on her. "We're working on a case together."

"Anything interesting?" came the joint reply.

"Yes, we just left the courthouse together, and that's why he asked for my home address yesterday. We were working on it last night."

The hazel gazes didn't waver.

"There's nothing personal going on between us."

"Of course not," was the immediate echo.

Christine nearly sighed, ready to concede she was fighting a losing battle. The twins would believe what they wanted to. She couldn't convince them otherwise. She only had to convince herself. "The brief?" she asked Mandy.

"Right here," the young blond responded, holding it up to follow Christine into her office as Christine flipped through the telephone messages she'd been handed. Watching her, Mandy shrugged. "Most of the calls were routine, but one might be a new client."

Interested immediately in the potential for growth, Christine set her briefcase down on her desk and smiled. "Good news."

Mandy's head bobbed agreement. "Job security. I think it might be a referral."

Setting the first three telephone memos aside as names she knew, Christine looked up at her secretary who stopped at the other side of the desk. "From who?"

"Don't know," Mandy shrugged. "The only thing he said was that he'd gotten your name from a friend, somebody you'd helped with a briefcase."

Christine's hand froze, and her stomach flipped. "Briefcase?"

"Uh-huh," Mandy confirmed. "Something about you having helped get it back to it's owner." Her shoulders moved again. "It didn't make a lot of sense to me, but he said you'd know what it was all about. Here's the brief."

Christine didn't speak as Mandy handed over the papers before disappearing back out the door. She couldn't. Her throat was locked with dread. And fear.

Yet anger rapidly took its place when she looked at the next message because she recognized the name even if Mandy didn't. It was another attorney. A man she knew by reputation only.

Mark Sherman.

Chapter 7

SPRING IN Los Angeles was warming towards summer, and David hoped the trail to Jimmy Wilson would soon be getting hot, too.

Passing the elevator to jog up the three flights to the office, he felt good about the network he had working on the search, and he had high hopes for results. His friends in the department, his acquaintances on the street were all reliable. And they didn't ask a lot of questions.

A few subtle comments, a hint of trouble for a well-liked judge, and the possibility of bringing someone bad down had some trusted contacts surfing the ears of the city to come up with some useable information. If he didn't get what he was looking for in the next twenty-four to forty-eight hours, it wouldn't be for want of trying.

His watch said it was just past four when he hit the hallway, and a few strides took him to and through the office door.

"Good day, ladies," he greeted before he was all the way inside and grinned when his call was answered by an echo of two. But Mandy was closer and moving fast—for the exit he'd just entered.

"Courthouse!" she called and ducked outside before the door slipped shut.

David turned to Candy. "Just you and me, kid."

"And Christine."

Reminded, he ignored the sudden surge of arousal, but he couldn't resist looking toward her office. The door was closed. That meant she was inside. Waiting for him.

The thought did odd things to his equilibrium, and it scrambled again hormones that had gone ballistic during the kiss. Frowning, he stepped silently forward to take the messages Candy was holding out to him and tried not to think about the embrace shared with Christine.

It had been a mistake. His, but the alternative would have been worse. He could have decked her. Or wrung her neck. Yet on a public street with too many witnesses, attempting manslaughter had been out of the question. Kissing her had been the only other option available, and he couldn't argue it'd been more pleasant than any of his other choices. Too much so.

"Anything urgent?" he asked Candy, barely glancing at the handwritten notes of calls she'd provided.

"No, but Christine wants to know when you arrive."

He grunted and glanced at the closed door again. Christine Dunn. Trouble with a capital T. It was time to get some distance back between them. "Give me a minute."

"Sure," Candy agreed with a grin he missed. "Take all the time you want."

He nodded, barely hearing her words, and slipped into his office to close the door quietly behind him. He had to get ready for the rendezvous at the parking structure, and he had to prepare himself to spend the next few hours with a woman he needed to avoid.

He sighed. She was stubborn. She wanted to be involved, and he understood the need. He also appreciated her dropping the guard she always hid behind to let him understand why, but that was part of the problem.

The excitement and the stress of the situation were exposing emotions, forcing trust and thrusting them together. He had to get them back apart because, once the kidnapping was solved and things calmed down, everything would have to go back to normal—and any intimacy spawned by the present circumstances would be regretted. By him and by her.

Dropping his messages on the desk, he shrugged out of his sports coat and headed to the washroom where, bending to splash water on his face, he stopped to confront himself in the mirror.

He was used to the patch, the sight of it, the necessity for it, and people's reactions to it. Stares of wonder, grimaces of sympathy, and looks of horror. Repulsion.

Never a vain man, his self-image had taken a beating over the last year, and he was still dealing with it. Perhaps always would be. The department shrink had told him to expect the fallout and more.

Depression, anger. He'd nearly been consumed by, before trying to drown both—along with himself—in a bottle, but his family's love had yanked him back from the brink. They still cared. He just didn't know if anyone else ever could. Or if he wanted them to.

His ventures into dating had been limited since the accident. Self-confidence shot, his buddies had been the first to throw him back into the intimate by-play of male-female relations, and for the most part, he'd survived the encounters intact.

Sighing he turned on the faucets to dip his hands into the warm flow. He'd healed on the outside, but he wasn't sure about the inside. Yet that wasn't the only problem standing between he and any attempt at romance.

One marriage had collapsed because of his chosen profession. Enforcing the law. The job held risks even out of uniform, and anyone he got permanently involved with would have to deal with those risks just as he would. The pressure was a heavy load to bear. He wasn't sure a woman existed who would be willing to carry the weight. Or if he wanted to find her if she did.

Did he really want to get back on the emotional roller coaster of commitment? He had himself to worry about. That and his work. It was enough. So were one night stands—something Christine Dunn, attorney at law, definitely was not.

She was the type of woman who got into a man's blood—which was okay as far as he was concerned. As long as it wasn't his, and he was determined it wouldn't be.

He'd take her out with him for the chase, maybe let her see how dangerous and iffy things could get, and if he scared her enough, she'd back off. And let him breathe.

He straightened to grab a towel. Still it was a shame. The kiss had been...tantalizing. A culmination could be even more so. They might make quite a team once she let her hair down, but she'd have to put it back up again—at the office they both shared and would have to share for some time to come.

That type of professional relationship rarely stood the strain of romantic liaisons and could have consequences he didn't want to deal with. Finding a new office, a new partner, a new start. It was all time consuming and unnecessary. That meant he had to keep the boundaries up.

Tossing the towel aside, he turned to swing back into the office and jerked to a halt when he saw her. The stranger. She was standing in the room, waiting for him, and she was in blue jeans and a black tee shirt.

Both hugged curves and molded skin with an intimacy that made his mouth water. Breasts, hips, thighs. All were accented. And her legs. Denim covered limbs that were long. Longer than he could have imagined. And slim. They seemed to go on forever.

He swallowed, wondering why she usually hid all of that behind suits and jackets.

"I knocked," Christine finally said when he continued to stare, and he nearly groaned. The road to hell was paved with good intentions, and she was going to make him crawl the entire way.

He cleared his throat and hoped his lips weren't covered in drool. "I had the water running," he told her and rapidly sought sanctuary by putting his back to her and going to his desk.

"I changed."

He winced. Did she think he hadn't noticed?

"Do you think this will be okay?"

Forced to turn to acknowledge her attire, he tried to keep his gaze levelled at her Nike clad feet. "Fine. As long as you're comfortable." And he wasn't. Still there was a good side to the alteration in her appearance. At least with her beside him, his senses would be on full alert.

"I'm ready to leave whenever you are," she told him. "Are we going early?"

"You bet," he assured her and took a deep breath before turning to face her, but he wasn't the only one who was nervous. She was, too. Fidgeting as he stared, he smothered a grin and decided to enjoy the moment. "You let your hair down."

Her hand immediately darted to the nape of her neck where the long blonde tresses had been woven into a braid that fell down her back to rest between her shoulder blades. "It seemed practical."

The grin escaped despite his best efforts. He couldn't help it. The word described her. Or at least who she wanted to be. He wasn't sure who she was yet. He didn't think she did either. "I've got to change, too."

If he'd drawn his gun from its holster on his belt, she wouldn't have jumped higher—or retreated faster. Stumbling back toward the door, she grappled for the handle. "Just call me when you're ready."

She vanished from sight, and he sighed. It didn't seem like she knew what to do with him any more than he did with her. That was a good thing. It would make keeping her at bay easier. And harder.

When she got perturbed, her eyes got bigger, and she blushed. Kind of cute. Intriguing. And tough to resist.

Muttering under his breath, he stalked back to the bathroom and the clothes he kept hanging inside. It was time to get into his biker wear of skull and cross bones and ratty jeans. Disguises were now part of his trade, and he'd need a good one over the next few hours if he was going to keep his interest under wraps from her.

CHRISTINE paced her office, unable to concentrate on the paperwork littering her desk. She was worried about the hours ahead, about what would happen and what wouldn't, about what might happen and might not. But at least David wasn't going to make it difficult.

He hadn't tried to talk her out of going with him again when she'd gone to see and to let him know she was ready. That surprised her. She'd expected he would. Just as she'd expected him to mention the kiss. But he hadn't.

Her teeth found her bottom lip. Afraid he would throw her momentary transgression in her face, she'd been prepared to give a little speech about professionalism and adulthood and resisting urges better left unacknowledged, but he hadn't given her the chance. Probably because he'd reached the same conclusion.

His reasonableness, she silently assured herself, was a relief. But, then, he'd always proven himself to be a reasonable man.

Smothering a groan, she muttered a self-deprecating reprimand. She didn't want to think about what a nice guy he was, about how different he could be from the other men she'd met. It was only necessary to remember, to remind herself, that they were business partners. Comrades. A team of two involved in cracking a case. No more.

Her fingers wound together in quiet agitation as she prowled the carpet. A stakeout. She'd never, in her wildest dreams, imagined she would ever go out on one. That subject wasn't covered in Lawyering 101 in law school. It didn't need to be because such activity was the milieu of the police, not attorneys, but at least, for the experience, she was going with him.

He was competent. He'd proven that the night before. When it came to the undercover stuff, David knew what he was doing. The phone call was something he'd been prepared for—more so than she—and he'd be as prepared for the meeting at the parking structure. She stopped pacing. Or at least she hoped he would be. He'd been behaving oddly in his office.

The way he'd stared at her. It was as if he'd never seen her before. The intensity of his gaze had jangled already dancing nerves, especially when just seeing him again had put her heart in her throat.

A delightful chill shook her from head to toe. His male aura was potent, his dark good looks heart stopping but, she abruptly assured herself resuming her pacing once more, ignorable.

Hard knuckles hit the wood of her door, and she nearly jumped out of her skin. Spinning, she faced his grin.

"Set to go?"

"Of course," she agreed with a huff that had her grabbing her purse from the desk and looking away from him. He was back in the black tee shirt again, and the holey jeans, too. As she followed him out the door and past a staring Candy, she couldn't help but notice the tear that remained positioned close to his left lower cheek. Through it she could actually get a glimpse of skin....

"This could be a long night."

Just thinking the same thing, she cleared her throat. "I'm ready," she insisted, but his gaze as he turned to look at her after hitting the button to call the elevator said he wasn't so certain. She lifted her chin in denial of his doubts. "I am."

The bell announcing the car's arrival rang, and he grunted. "Maybe I'm not."

Shocked by his lack of confidence, her mouth worked as the doors slid open, but he avoided the question by stepping inside. She hastily followed. "What do you mean?"

He swung to face her, the doors closed once more, and abruptly alone with him, she realized how small the elevator was and how easy it would be to just reach out and touch him. As she watched, his gaze dropped to skim her form. "I'm not used to having a female partner."

The temperature in the car started to rise, and she gulped in air that suddenly seemed in short supply. "I'm not used to having a partner period."

His lips twitched. "Is that supposed to make me feel better?"

"It means we're both operating at a disadvantage."

He grunted. "You'll never know."

She frowned, uncertain of what to say and studied him as he lifted his head to watch the numbers of the floors light and die. Out of his suit coat and in a loose tee shirt and jeans, he appeared relaxed and abruptly out of uniform.

He wore no jacket to cover a holster or the firearm she assumed he usually carried—a revolver he could and would protect them with during the coming hours if need be. She swallowed apprehension. Was he unarmed? Had he left his weapon behind in the office? Were they going into battle unable to defend themselves?

"Didn't you bring your gun?"

Her blurted question made his lips twitch as he leaned negligently against the wall, his one hand tucked into a pocket just under the hem of the shirt. "Why? Do you want to shoot somebody?"

"Don't tempt me," she snapped irritably. "I was just wondering if you had it with you in case something happened."

"It's right here," he said, flipping up the tee shirt to expose the holster snapped to the belt of his jeans—along with an intriguing glimpse of bronze skin dusted with dark hair.

She sucked in her breath to steady the sudden pound of blood in her ears that had more to do with warm flesh than cold steel.

"Don't worry," he told her as the bell rang again, and the car came to a halt once more. "I'll protect you."

"I can protect myself," she sniffed and led the way out of the elevator into the underground garage.

"Really?" he asked, cocking an eyebrow at her. "How? Did you bring your cat?"

She sputtered, and he strode away, leaving her to scramble after him toward a battered brown Chevy. "I'll have you know that I took karate."

He stopped to stick the key in the driver's door and eyed her over the roof of the car when she went around to wait on the passenger's side. "One of those eight-week courses where the instructor teaches you how to kick a man in the balls?"

She smiled sweetly. "No, the knee cap. Want me to demonstrate?"

"No thanks." He ducked inside and she jerked the door open when he leaned over to flip the lock, but if she had anything else to say, he wasn't wasting any time on idle conversation. Before she was even climb inside, the engine rumbled to life with a reassuring purr that spoke of hidden power under the hood.

Slamming her door shut, butterflies danced in her stomach, and the clock on the dash caught her eye. "We'll be there early."

"Not a problem. We want some time to get the lay of the land," he said, backing the car out of its space and guiding it competently toward the exit. "And it'll give us a chance to talk."

"Good," she agreed. "We need to. I haven't had a chance to tell you about my phone call."

"What phone call?"

"The one from Mark Sherman."

Brakes squealed, the car came to a screeching halt, and only fast reflexes saved her from a collision with the waiting windshield.

But before she had a chance to right herself, his hand was on her shoulder hauling her back against the seat.

"What?" he demanded, glaring at her in the shadows of the Chevy.

"He called while we were at the courthouse."

"Then you didn't talk to him," David sighed.

"Of course, I did," she denied. "I called him back."

David groaned, and his head dropped to the steering wheel. "You couldn't wait for me?"

She scowled. "All we did was talk."

"What he said could have been incriminating. We could have gotten it on tape."

"Wire tapping's illegal," she objected primly. "Besides, we didn't talk long. He wants to meet."

David started the car moving forward again, out of the garage and onto the street. "Did you set a date?"

"Tomorrow."

He swore. Profusely, but she wasn't intimidated.

"We don't have a lot of time."

David's fingers drummed the steering wheel. "I won't be able to go with you."

She nodded, swallowing her doubts. "I know."

Silence fell, dark and gloomy despite the sunshine pouring through the windows. He broke it with a sigh. "I think you should postpone it."

"Why?"

"We need time to do some research," he insisted, edging the car along with the barely moving traffic. Rush hour was underway once more. "Besides, you don't want your name linked with him, Chris. He's scum. If you're seen associating with him, your reputation's going to get shot to hell."

Unexpectedly moved by his concern for her, she nodded reluctantly. "I know. That's why I asked him to come to my office."

David's jaw dropped, and halting at a red light, a lopsided grin curved his mouth. "You know, counselor. You might be better at this secret agent stuff than I thought."

She smiled, more pleased than she should have been at his compliment, but she didn't think about the whys. She just enjoyed the warmth of his appreciation on the short ride to the parking garage.

Only a mile or so away, the time it took to get there had more to do with the number of cars on the street than on the distance they had to travel, but arrival at their destination wasn't the end of their journey. Once inside the looming structure boasting several floors available for parking, they still had to get to the top, and sitting beside him, her mouth went dry with anticipation as level after level disappeared behind and below them.

What would they find when they got there? Who would be waiting? She didn't know. She wasn't sure she even wanted to know, but it was too late for doubts. Or regrets. Yet surprise brought unexpected relief when, emerging into sunlight once more, she recognized the first vehicle they saw.

"A red pick up!"

"I see it," he assured her but made no attempt to stop anywhere near the apparently empty four by four. Instead he drove past it and into a vacant spot further down from where the vehicle sat exposed and alone in the corner and not far from the stairwell that housed steps and an elevator as an easy means of getting back to the ground floor.

"What are we doing to do?" she asked, eying the pickup out the back window.

Instead of following her gaze, he handed her a pair of wraparound sunglasses before leaning past her to reach into the back seat to retrieve a leather jacket. "We're going to act like anyone else who drives into a parking lot and parks. We're going to get out and leave."

"Leave! We can't!" she started to protest, but her words were lost when he threw open his door, stepped outside and left her behind. Irritated, edgy, swearing at him and men in general, she jammed the glasses on her nose and rushed out to meet him by the trunk—and nearly squealed when his arm snaked out to bring her hip crashing unexpectedly against his.

"Relax, girl friend," he murmured, lowering his head to her ear. "And play the part. We're going to saunter over to that exit by the truck and go inside to grab the elevator. Got it?"

She didn't even try to answer. She couldn't. Not with her right side plastered against his left and the heat from his body branding hers. The only thing she could do was hang on, but that was okay. She needed the support.

Suddenly confronted with the unknown, her knees were knocking, and a chill was in the air. It was tinged with fear. Being next to him was the only way to stay warm. And safe.

Letting her arm fall around his waist, she licked dry lips and tried to find her voice. If appearances were important, it would seem natural for them to be in conversation, but her vocal chords were frozen. And, as they approached the truck, so were her lungs.

Was someone inside? Watching? Waiting? What if whoever was driving the truck recognized her? Him? Them?

Yet if she was worried, David didn't seem to be. His motions, his actions, were as fluid and natural as he walked as any other day, and she strove desperately to copy his rhythmic motions. It was a relief when they finally stepped into the cement cubicle containing the elevator and stairwell, but the charade didn't end there as she expected.

"Let's take the stairs, babe," he announced loudly, and too

surprised to protest, she followed him when he yanked open the steel door leading to the steps.

"What..?" she began once inside and isolated from any possible prying eyes or ears, but he wasn't standing still long enough to talk.

Immediately releasing her, he took off for the floors below. "Come on!"

Left with little choice and no chance to argue, she scampered after him. No way was she letting him out of her sight, but gaining speed as he hurried past two levels, she nearly slammed into him when he stopped without warning at the next door. He pulled it open and stepped through. "Where are you going?" she demanded, right on his heels, but he held up a hand to silence her and pulled a cell phone from his jacket pocket.

He rapidly punched in a series of numbers. "It's me. I've got a make and license."

Her jaw dropped in amazement as she listened to him rattle off the year, make, model and license number to the red truck. How he could have seen and absorbed all of that information with the single glance she'd seen him give the vehicle, she didn't know, but a more pressing concern was the person on the other end of the call. She wasn't the only one working with him on the case. He had somebody else on the outside, and he hadn't bothered to clue her in to a third party's involvement.

"Someone's inside the cab, and I think they've got company on the same floor," he concluded and broke the line.

"You have somebody else helping you," she accused, crossing her arms to glare at him.

"Honey, I'm not Superman. I don't have x-ray vision, and I can't be in two places at the same time," he answered with a shrug. "If this gets dicey, I'm going to need back up in pursuit."

"You could have told me."

"I am telling you," he assured her, suddenly closer than she realized.

She took a step backwards.

He grinned in appreciation of her retreat. "Do I make you nervous, counselor?"

"This situation makes me nervous," she denied, lifting her chin to a haughty angle. "What happens now?"

"My guess is that whoever's in the red truck will join his pals in the other car they have sitting up top."

"I didn't see anyone," she murmured, impressed and intimidated at the same time. She hadn't noticed anybody in the pickup or anywhere else on the roof of the building. But, then, she hadn't seen him look around either.

"That's why I'm here," he pointed out and continued. "I think they'll wait for the judge, watch for the drop, make sure no one else is anywhere nearby and then snatch, grab and run."

"They don't trust him," she murmured. "This is another test."

"It's a continuation of the same quiz they had him take this morning," David denied. "When it comes to Wilson, they have to be cautious. He's a friend of the police. The bad guys have to make sure he's on their side and that he's not setting them up."

She nodded. "What do we do until then?"

"I'm sure we can think of something."

The heat in his gaze sent a shiver down her spine—and made her want to run. Fast. He was too dangerous for her peace of mind. Something he could destroy with a kiss, but he stopped her plotted escape by holding out his hand.

"Trust me, Chris."

She hesitated before putting her palm to his, but she didn't regret giving in to his request when she complied. The warmth of his skin against hers was comforting, and the strength of his fingers around hers reassuring. "I do trust you."

"Good girl," he whispered and brought her to his side and into the stairwell once more to call the elevator.

TRAFFIC WAS still moving slow when David led Christine back across the street to the garage a short time later. Rush hour was dragging on, but he wasn't as concerned with it as he was her. She hadn't let go of his hand. Not since he'd offered it to her, and the way she clutched his fingers said her nerves were still dancing. Yet being nervous kept her thinking, and keeping her off balance stopped her from being afraid.

What they were about to do wasn't that dangerous. At least not if they didn't get caught, and he didn't think they would.

"What kind of car does the judge drive?" he asked as they waited for the elevator that groaned with each turn of the pulley. He already knew the answer, but he didn't know if she did.

"A silver Buick," she answered, a tremor making her arm vibrate against his.

"You're doing fine," he told her and watched her eyes lift to his. They were wide and blue above the glasses that kept slipping down her nose, and they were filled with uncertainty. He squeezed her fingers in reassurance, finding he liked the excuse to hang on to her. "When we get upstairs, we're going to just amble back to the car."

Anxiously she lifted her left arm to glance at her watch. "It's not six yet. Do you think he'll be on time?"

"Of course," David guaranteed without hesitation and ushered her into the empty and graffiti-stained elevator when the doors opened. "Judges are always on schedule. It's the attorneys who are late."

Her head shot up, and he smiled at her glare.

"Just wanted to see if I had your attention, counselor," he murmured and reached out to push the glasses back up her nose as the elevator grumbled a protest before beginning the laborious climb back to the upper most floor of the structure.

"You have it."

"Good." He released her hand to wrap an arm around her shoulders. The action brought her against his side once more, and she didn't protest. She just molded herself against him as if she belonged there, and it was a sensation he liked.

He enjoyed touching her. Being touched by her.

Abruptly swearing under his breath at his wandering imagination, he glared at the numbers above the doors that reflected the floors as they passed them. She was making him lose his concentration. That wasn't a good thing. Not if he was going to do his job—and keep her safe while he was doing it. "Just stay beside me," he ordered brusquely. "Walk slow and easy. Timing is critical."

"We want to be in our car when the judge arrives?"

"We want to be leaving as he's coming because out of sight is out of mind."

She nodded understanding. "If we're gone, they'll only be watching him and not us."

"They'll be thinking that we're history."

"But we'll be waiting outside," she suggested. "But not for the red truck."

"You catch on quick," he agreed. "The red pickup is a decoy. Probably stolen. It's the black van we'll be after."

The van in question was still parked on the roof when they stepped out into the quickly fading rays of the day's sun moments later. He figured it was occupied while the red truck was now empty. The bait was out, the hook was in. The blackmailers just needed to wait and see if they were going to be able to reel anything in. Like a judge trying to save his son.

"Walk slow," he murmured and she mirrored his steps, but staying close to him meant her breast kept rubbing against his chest. The motion provided more distraction than he needed or wanted. Gritting his teeth, he nearly sighed in relief when they reached the Chevy.

She moved immediately around to the passenger side. He, on the other hand, didn't rush to get in the car. Casually shrugging into the leather jacket he'd been carrying, he adjusted the collar and took the time to look around as if admiring the sunset. The light was glinting off the mountains of glass that were the buildings of Los Angeles, but if he appeared to be daydreaming, he was really waiting. Biding his time.

"Ready to go?" he finally asked her over the roof of the Chevy.

Her answering smile was tight but would, he knew, appear natural from a distance. "Ready as I'll ever be."

He nodded and unlocked the door to duck inside. In less than a minute, she was sitting beside and looking at him with eyes filled with uncertainty. He could almost see her heart in her throat and hear its pounding. "Almost time."

The dash board clock confirmed his statement when he turned the key in the ignition. Two minutes before six, and as the digital numbers jumped ahead to five fifty-nine, a silver Buick came up the ramp.

David put the Chevy in reverse and headed for the exit. He was on his way down the ramp when Judge Wilson pulled his car to a halt and climbed out of his Buick with the briefcase. David saw both in his rear view mirror. "He's making the drop."

And everything went like clock work as he guided the Chevy down to the ground floor. He found an empty stall and was able to wait long enough for the judge to catch up and pass them, and he was on the street in traffic minutes later when the black van pulled out of the garage and into the lane a few cars behind them.

His lips curved in anticipation of the coming pursuit. "Got 'em!"

A strangled sound came from the seat beside him. It reminded him that he wasn't alone. Turning his head, he caught Christine looking out the back window. "Eyes forward, Chris."

Her Adam's apple bobbed in her throat as she quickly looked forward, but if she was anxious, he wasn't.

"No worries, partner. This is when the fun begins."

The look she gave him was incredulous, but playing cat and mouse was something he'd rapidly learned to enjoy after getting his private investigator's license. The hunt, the chase, the capture. It was all part of the game. One he liked. A lot. And it was one he hoped he was getting good at as traffic lights changed and the van stayed in line behind him.

Quickly grabbing the phone from his pocket, he punched redial. “He’s going my way. Jump ahead to Alameda.”

Knowing his friend would comply, the connection between the two of them broke, and a mild form of bumper tag began.

Staying ahead of the van, he tried to anticipate the driver’s next turn, but eventually, he let the van pass. In early evening traffic, he didn’t need to worry about it getting away from him or the other retired cop he had with him on the road and on the van’s tail. The remnants of rush hour were keeping everyone at a snail’s pace.

Yet when the streets bordered by skyscrapers and businesses were left behind, the van picked up speed, and pursuit took on a hide-and-seek aspect as the driver made a few well-chosen turns.

It quickly became clear the neighborhoods those inside the van were heading for did not cater to the elite. Beyond the windshield, the price of real estate gradually plummeted. Broken glass took the place of bay windows, manicured lawns disappeared under piles of trash, and traffic decreased significantly with the change in venue.

Following at a discreet distance, David fell back but kept the van in sight as he punched redial on his cell phone once more. “I’ve got him. Let’s part ways and chat tomorrow about what you find on the license plates.”

A grunt of agreement was his answer, and he hung up and turned the Chevy right down a parallel block to avoid detection. Yet, with dusk gathering, the van and its occupants seemed oblivious to all except where they were going, and precautions appeared unnecessary. Still David remained cautious, especially when headlights started coming on around him.

Loss of daylight was going to make tailing harder. His best hope was for the van to reach its destination before total darkness fell and before he had to flick his beams on, too. And, with no warning, an unexpected crank of the steering wheel gave him his wish.

The black vehicle bumped into an alleyway and disappeared.

David didn’t attempt to follow. Instead he took the Chevy immediately to the curb, shut off the engine and reached for the door handle. The alley had to mean the van was stopping, and a halt would see the briefcase transferred. He needed to be close to see where it went next.

“What do we do now?”

He nearly jumped out of his skin at the question. Intent on the chase, concentrating on his mission, he'd forgotten all about Christine. She'd remained silent since leaving the parking structure.

"You stay here," he ordered and jumped out of the car.

He saw her mouth open to object, but he had no time to say more. Explanations would have to wait, and any belief that his directive was an attempt at male domination needed to be ignored. For the moment, only the briefcase mattered.

Hustling down the sidewalk, the pace he set wasn't fast enough to draw attention to himself but was quick enough to get him to where he wanted to go in a hurry. The alley entrance.

Pausing briefly, glancing around swiftly, he stepped inside.

Almost at once he heard voices. They echoed from up ahead. The men from the van were talking and moving, but in the darkness that had fallen to cloak the city, with the clutter of dumpsters and the uneven jutting of walls and fences, he couldn't see it or them. He had to get closer.

Edging forward, he stayed in the shadows and out of sight, but stealth proved to be poor cover. A noise echoed. It was followed by a muffled step. Both came from behind him.

Flattening himself against a building wall, David held his breath. Somebody was in the alley with him. And they were right on his tail.

Chapter 8

DAVID DUCKED behind a dumpster. A lookout on the street, watching the alley, was coming to check him out.

Silently he cursed his luck and his haste. If he hadn't been in such a hurry to go after the briefcase, he wouldn't have missed the guard. Quietly he eased the trapped air from his lungs. Now he was going to have to deal with the consequences.

Another muffled footstep sounded. It was accompanied by ragged breathing. Whoever was behind him was close. And cautious. But David was ready.

A silhouette appeared. He lurched, grabbed a fistful of material, and threw. His shadow ricocheted into the wall, and David went after him, shoving his revolver up against the man's nose.

But it wasn't a man. It was a woman.

"What the hell are you doing here?"

Christine's mouth moved at his harsh demand, but no words came out. And he wasn't surprised. She was terrified. Even in the dark he could see the blood had drained from her face, and he could feel the fierce hammer of her heart. It was slamming erratically against the forearm he had braced across her breasts and was using to pin her to the bricks.

He growled, not feeling particularly sympathetic, and let her go. If she was afraid, she deserved to be. Sneaking up on him like that. But removing his arm left nothing to hold her up. He had to catch her when her knees gave out.

Air whistled back into her lungs on a squeak as he propped her back up against the wall, and grumbling darkly and striving for patience, he tried to remind himself that he'd scared the daylights out of her. Not that her unexpected appearance had done his pulse rate any good.

"Are you all right?" he managed to ask through gritted teeth, sorry he'd frightened her but not feeling guilty about it. Not while standing in a black alley.

She nodded, and he sighed in disgust.

"You don't take orders very well."

"Maybe you shouldn't give them," she stammered.

"I didn't have time to discuss the situation."

She recovered her poise enough to sniff indignantly. "I'm quite capable of making snap decisions when given the opportunity."

Muttering curses he didn't care if she heard, he hissed at her. "Fine. Wonderful. Next time the bad guys are about to disappear with the loot, I'll remember that."

She opened her mouth, and he held up a warning finger.

"Not another word. Just shut up, and stay behind me."

Her scowl spoke volumes, but he ignored it and her and turned back to the search. If there was anything left to find.

Silently berating the entire female population for its interference and her in particular for her hard headedness, he continued his approach around the chaos of the alley. He wanted to get where he'd heard the voices and to where he hoped the van was still stopped. If it was gone, it was lost and so was the money in the briefcase—not to mention any lead they might have gotten on the judge's son.

An indecipherable gurgle came from behind him.

He spun in alarm. "What?"

"I stepped on something."

Something disgusting from the tone of her voice, but he didn't care. "Then watch where you're going."

He swung back to what lay ahead, and she fell silent. For about thirty seconds.

"Now what?" he snarled. And in the blackness he saw her wave a hand in front of her nose.

"It stinks."

It did. He just hadn't noticed, but being a cop had taken him to all sorts of interesting and less than exotic places. And each had proven to have its own unique smell. He leaned close to her. "Then hold your breath."

She glared, and he grinned. Through clenched teeth.

Leaving her to follow him around a rusty and dented dumpster, a lump on the cement that looked suspiciously like a pair of legs made him pause—and her inhale sharply.

"Is he dead?" she whispered in hushed horror.

David shook his head, catching a whiff of cheap liquor. "No, just drunk so don't step on him—and be quiet!"

"All right!" she snapped back.

He curled his lips at her and left her to keep up with him as he crept to the corner of another building. Slipping to the end of the battered brick, he dared a peek around the wall and saw the van.

Immediately he sank to a squat to study it and the surroundings.

Thankfully, there could be no doubt as to where the briefcase had gone. Only one door was anywhere nearby, and it was on the loading dock the vehicle was parked next to.

The big wooden ramp was what had prevented him from seeing the van from the street. Set in from the otherwise straight line of the alley, the dock was back farther than the other buildings to allow space for any delivery trucks to maneuver when dropping off goods. That was why the van had seemed to disappear. The driver had slipped it right up next to the dock and the cement steps leading inside.

"Is that it?"

The quiet query came from over his shoulder, and he nodded. "That's it. And no one's in sight. They all went inside." Which was a shame. He would have liked to see a few faces to compare to some mug shots.

"Are we just going to sit out here?" she prodded minutes later when he hadn't moved.

Exasperated, his gaze met hers as she stooped behind him. "This isn't Hollywood, counselor, and I'm not Arnold Schwarzenegger. Bullets don't bounce off my chest."

"But we can't see anything from outside," she protested in a belligerent whisper.

"We see where the van's parked. That gives us an address and eventually an owner."

"Who might be helping Sherman?"

"Gold star, counselor. Go to the head of your class." Ignoring her sharp intake of breath and certain no one from the van was out and about, he stood with a sigh and shoved the gun he was still holding back into its holster under his tee shirt.

"Now what?" she asked, straightening, too.

"We go back."

She stared. "What? That's it? That's all we do?"

"You want me to go in with guns blazing and demand they tell me where the kid is?"

She shrugged. "Couldn't you just go in and ask?"

He groaned and stepped past her, dragging a hand through his hair. "I'm out of here—and you're not ever coming with me again."

"Why?"

"Because you ask too many questions." He spun back to face her without warning and, not prepared for his abrupt change in direction, she collided with his chest. "Take a look around, Miss Dunn. You're not in a court room any more."

"So? Nothing happened."

"It could have," he said, jabbing a finger against her collar bone. "Or did you like the feel of steel against your nostril?"

She sputtered, and he turned away and froze.

Three shadows had appeared in the moonlight. Three men, and they were blocking the way out of the alley. He didn't have to ask to know they meant trouble. He put out a hand to push Christine behind him.

"Out for a walk?" one of the trio asked, stepping forward and into the muted light filtering in from the street. It illuminated his face, a maze of sharp planes and angles, and his body was long and lanky with youth. With hair cropped short, his nose was pierced, and a tatoo of a dragon breathed fire on the side of one biceps while a leopard roared on the other.

"Meeting a friend who didn't show up," David responded, letting his arms fall loosely to his sides. "Maybe you've seen him."

"Don't know," the second said, moving to join his friend in the dim glow from too distant street lamps. He was as young as the first but broader, and his head was shaved to stubble. Yet it was what he had in his hand that made David's pulse flutter. A switch blade. It gleamed cruelly in the night. "What's he look like?"

Fear shuddered through David. His nightmare of meeting cold metal again in an alley was repeating itself once more. Struggling silently against dread, he shrugged. "Short, dark, sells what makes you happy."

"You looking for a fix?" the first asked and grinned at the second. "That means the man has cash, Zip."

"And a babe, T.K.," the third agreed, speaking for the first time but staying in the shadows. "Think he'll share?"

David felt Christine tremble, and her terror abruptly erased his own. She needed him to protect her. Without him, she was defenseless, vulnerable, but he wasn't about to let her become a victim. Forgetting sharp steel, he smiled a less than congenial warning. "What I've got, I keep."

"We'll see," Zip said stepping forward, blade held ready, and when he charged, Christine screamed.

David shoved her aside and dodged. Years of training kept him calm, and a surge of anger gave him strength and cunning. Using Zip's momentum, he sent the hoodlum crashing into a dumpster before spinning to sink his fist into an approaching T.K.'s ribs. The gang's leader doubled over and left David free to confront the third member of the group who began to circle warily.

Having taken the advantage by drawing first blood, David played it cautious. He was still outnumbered. T.K. was staggering, but Zip was swearing and ready to come again. Feinting to the left, David dipped right, pivoted on the ball of one foot and sent the other into the third's abdomen.

Breath whooshed from startled lungs, but David didn't allow time to recover. He brought both fists down on stooped shoulders and sent the third man to the ground. But that left him exposed.

Zip dashed forward with a vicious swipe of his blade. It caught leather and skin, and David cringed as pain lanced up his arm. Yet he forgot it. He had to because Zip was coming in again.

Jumping aside, the knife missed, but T.K. didn't. Unexpectedly charging back into the fray to grapple hand-to-hand, his entrance knocked Zip out of the way and caught David by surprise.

Hard knuckles found his ribs. David staggered but didn't step back. Holding his ground, he blocked where he could and threw some punches of his own. Even still a fist got through his defenses. Connecting with his jaw, the blow knocked his head back. Yet if the strike rattled his teeth, it didn't do any damage. It just made him mad. And more determined.

Harder than T.K., more solid in build, he bided his time and absorbed what punishment the young hoodlum tried to dish out—until the opening he was waiting for came.

His short jab connected where it counted. T.K. grunted and reeled back, suddenly taking more abuse than he was giving out, and Zip roared in frustration as David maneuvered to keep T.K. in between them. Yet T.K. didn't last much longer. A final pop to the jaw, and he dropped.

Zip nearly tripped over his pal in his eagerness to get the kill, and David took advantage of the clumsy approach.

Pivoting away, he kicked out. Zip darted out of reach and swore again. Loudly. David motioned him forward, egging him on, and Zip snarled and slashed. The knife caught leather but not skin.

Behind him, David heard Christine whimper and then saw her move out of the corner of his eye—just as T.K. tried to get back to his feet.

The clang of metal told him that she'd used a garbage can lid as a battering ram. Probably on T.K.'s head. David grinned at Zip. The odds were now in his favor because the third man had never gotten to his feet again.

Zip tried a head ram. Clutching the knife, he put his head down and barreled straight into David's midsection. The idea was to grab hold and stick the blade in, but David caught Zip's wrist and didn't let go as they both tumbled to the pavement.

The impact shook them both. It nearly knocked them apart, but Zip was tenacious if not skilled. And his determination to stay in the game gave David the leverage he needed.

With Zip sprawled, legs apart as he wrestled for control, David brought his knee straight up into Zip's groin. Zip howled agony and dropped the knife.

David didn't hesitate. Grabbing the discarded weapon, he rolled clear and jumped to his feet, but the cold feel of steel in his hand was tempting. It gave the illusion of power along with the ability to kill, and with adrenaline pounding in his veins, his fingers closed around the handle in a tight fist before he stepped toward Zip to test the metal's strength.

Christine immediately leapt forward to grab his arm. "David! No!"

He barely heard and easily shook her off.

"David!" she cried again and shoved her way in front of him. "Stop it!"

Forced to look at her, unable to move with her hands planted against his chest, he halted. But he didn't back up.

"David, listen to me!" she argued, pushing against him with determined strength. "He's not worth it!"

Her shouted declaration made him blink, and her insistence penetrated the angry fog surrounding him.

"Put the knife away, David."

Glancing down at the weapon he held, David stared in startled recognition, and his grip eased.

Christine sighed her relief and captured his gaze with hers. "Let's just leave him here with the rest of the garbage."

"Bitch!" Zip swore from where he writhed on the ground, and the oath made her eyes narrow.

Slowly, she let David go with an order. "Stay here."

Curious, rage fading, he did as she said and watched her move to the side of the alley and the debris scattered there. A brief search brought what she was apparently looking for. A smelly crate. Lifting and carrying it back to his side, she hoisted it in the air before dumping the stinking contents all over Zip.

She dropped the crate as Zip's curses rent the air. "Like I said, let's just leave him here with the rest of the garbage." She glanced up at David. "We can go now."

Grinning as she abruptly spun on her heel and walked away, head held high, he looked down at Zip as the fallen man groaned. "The lady's tougher than she looks." And intrigued by the vague sway of jeaned hips in the night, he pocketed the switchblade and went after her.

"WE DON'T HAVE to do this," David protested as Christine pushed him through her condo door less than an hour later.

"Yes, we do," she insisted, not about to let him out of her sight before she saw to the blood on his lip and otherwise assured herself that he was all right. She knew too well that part of men's arrogance was their belief in their invincibility. They'd as soon fall flat on their face as admit they were hurt—or take proper care of that hurt. "Go sit down."

Mumbling, he did as she said, and she retreated to the kitchen for ice before going to the bathroom for a clean wash cloth and some antiseptic.

Why her hands weren't trembling as she wet the cloth, she didn't know. She'd been scared to death. Still was. When the man called Zip had charged with that knife ...

She shut off the water and swallowed hard. If she'd been frightened of that sharp steel, she couldn't imagine what David had felt. He had, after all, lost an eye to a blade, and that thought couldn't have been far from his mind during the fight. Regardless, he'd fought with confidence, strength and terrifying brutality. And he'd won. Thank God.

Carrying her armful of supplies back down the hall to the living room, she heard someone talking and realized it was David—speaking to Arthur, her cat. She smiled at the sight of the two of them going nose-to-nose. "He doesn't usually come out for strangers."

"We're not strangers," David protested. "We spent the night together."

She rolled her eyes and set the supplies down and gasped when she looked to him once more. He'd shrugged out of the leather jacket he'd been wearing, and the blood on his lip was nothing compared to the stream of red drying on his biceps. "David!"

He followed her stare with a shrug. "It's nothing. Just a scratch."

"Scratch!"

He glanced warily from it to her. "You're not going to faint, are you?"

"I don't faint."

He sighed. "That's a relief."

When he sank down onto the chair, she grabbed the cloth and knelt beside him, pausing to grimace at the ugly wound. "You might need stitches."

"No, what I need is a drink."

She dabbed, and he flinched. "Hold still."

"Easy for you to say," he growled.

"If you'd used your gun, this wouldn't have happened," she retorted.

"I didn't want to make any noise."

She stared at him.

"Bullets make noise," he clarified. "And I didn't want those guys in the van coming back outside."

"In case they made the connection between us and them."

"Exactly."

She went back to cleaning the wound. It looked nasty. "I have some Tylenol."

"I'd prefer bourbon."

"I have wine."

"That'll do," he agreed and smiled when she stopped what she was doing to narrow her eyes on him.

"Fine," she said, standing and shoving the ice at him. "Put that on your lip. If it swells, none of the ladies will think you're pretty any more."

"You think I'm pretty?"

On her way to the kitchen, she stopped to look back at him and into his wondering grin. "You have your charms."

His grin got wider. "Flattery will get you anything you want."

Her heart skipped, but she kept her gaze steady. "The ice."

He jammed it immediately against his mouth, and she nearly laughed. He was bleeding, probably exhausted, and he was still ready to make fun of himself.

It didn't take long to get the wine. In minutes she was on her way back to the living room with a full glass of rose colored liquid, but when she arrived, it was to find him examining the leather coat. It had several slashes in it. All in vital places.

"I think I need a new one," he told her with regret.

A chill shivered down her spine as, laying the jacket back on his lap, she handed him the glass. “You were lucky.”

“We were.”

Dipping some antiseptic on a piece of gauze, she bit her lip. “I shouldn’t have followed you. I know.”

“But you don’t take orders well.”

“No, I don’t,” she admitted without hesitation and turned to gently press the cotton to the wound.

Air hissed through his teeth, and he grimaced at her. “Especially from men.”

She lifted her gaze to his.

“Not all men are dictators,” he told her softly. “Some of us are real wimps.”

She couldn’t stop the curve of her lips and used her free hand to make him put the ice back to his mouth. “You’re not a wimp.” Looking away from him, she shook her head in silent wonder. “Or a dictator. You’ve always been fair with me. I was just scared. I didn’t want to be alone in the car.”

“First stakeout,” he sympathized. “Nerves.”

“At least I was able to help.”

He nodded. “The garbage lid.”

“And you know karate, too.”

“A little bit,” he conceded, and her smile lingered when she recognized the humor in his gaze.

“You didn’t kick him in the knee.”

“Nope. I went for a home run.”

Frowning at the wound she hoped was clean, she sat back on her heels to look at him. “Do you think they’ll try that with anyone else after what happened?”

“They’ll probably think twice,” he assured her and held up the knife he’d taken from Zip. It was folded safely in its sheath. “Want a souvenir?”

“I don’t know how to use it.”

“I don’t either,” he admitted. “I’m not fond of blades.”

Her fingers brushed his as she took it from him, and unspoken warmth passed between them. And understanding. “Thank you for protecting me.”

Not removing the ice from his lip, he kept his eye on her. “My pleasure.”

But even if he wasn’t touching her, she felt the heat. It radiated from him to her, and the strength of it startled. Quickly she retreated from it and him by grabbing the gauze to wrap it carefully around his torn flesh. "You've lost a lot of blood."

"Probably looks worse than it is."

Setting the tape aside in favor of the wet cloth once more, she began washing away the dried blood that had run down his arm. "You can sleep on my couch."

"That's becoming a habit."

Her pulse jumped, but she kept her eyes on her task. Yet cleaning his skin, feeling the hard muscle of his forearm beneath her hands was suddenly making it difficult to breathe.

"Christine."

She jerked at the sound of her name, and his finger found her chin to make sure she couldn't avoid looking at him any longer. "I ..." she started to stammer, but he shook his head and leaned closer.

"Sometimes its better to be seen and not heard."

She murmured, ready to protest, but words were lost when his mouth brushed hers.

A butterfly's touch, the caress teased, stirred, and she trembled when he backed away to hover a hair's breadth away.

"This isn't a good idea."

"You're telling me," he agreed, and his lips found hers again. More firmly this time and with more urgency, he pulled her into the embrace, and she wasn't ready to resist. In fact, she preferred to give in.

Letting him draw her closer, her hands lifted to his shoulders, and his buried themselves in her hair. The already broken braid fell apart, and the blonde mass tumbled loose to become a playground for his fingers.

"Silk," he told her, nipping with clever teeth, but the flexing of sinew and muscle beneath her palms reminded her of steel. Smooth, strong and finely honed.

He tried to turn his head away to explore new territory, but she coaxed him back. His mouth fused with hers again, the kiss deepened, and he unexpectedly yipped.

Surprised she drew away and watched him wince and put a finger to the cut the ice had been soothing.

"Ouch."

She tucked her tongue against her cheek to stop her laugh. "I thought real men didn't admit pain."

"If you're going to be insulting, I'm going to leave," he mumbled and flexed his jaw where hard knuckles had hit. "Besides," he sighed, grabbing her by the waist and putting her carefully from him. "I think you'd be safer if I didn't spend the night here."

Heat rushed into her cheeks at his blatant stare. "But ..."

"Don't tempt fate, counselor. We survived one skirmish tonight, let's get some rest before we begin another."

He stood, and following him to his feet, she suddenly felt incredibly small and vulnerable beside him. She wasn't sure she liked the feeling. She wasn't sure she didn't either.

"You'll have to take a taxi in the morning," he told her, turning toward the hall and the front door, but he stopped to scratch Arthur who'd been watching the human tussle with blinking feline wisdom.

"I don't mind."

"And I won't be in right away," he continued, releasing the cat to look at her. "I need to check some sources."

It was on the tip of her tongue to ask what, who and where, but she swallowed the urge. He'd proven she could trust him. More than once. When and if he knew anything, he'd tell her. "Okay."

"What time's your meeting with Sherman?"

"Just after noon."

David frowned, the expression lining his face with dark disapproval. "Will you reschedule it?"

"I'll tell him my secretary forgot to write down a hearing date on my calendar."

He smiled, and her toes curled.

"When should I tell him we'll meet?"

"How about Monday? That gives us time to dig."

She nodded. "Is there anything else I can do?"

"Not unless you know someone who might be able to give you some dirt on Sherman."

Chewing at her lip, she considered. "There's a court clerk who's prone to talk if someone wants to stand and listen."

His gaze shone with approval, and a friendly knuckle clipped her jaw. "I'll meet you in the office tomorrow as soon as I can."

"I'll be waiting," she assured him and stilled when heat erupted again. It surged into the space between them, filling it rapidly like lava dripping from a bubbling volcano. One step would take her into his smoldering magma.

"Get some rest."

His gruff order followed him out of her home, but it was a minute before she could breathe. Think. Because if he was gone. He didn't have to be. She would have let him stay.

Quickly moving to the door he'd just passed through, she threw the bolt lock and rattled the security chain into place, but she didn't feel safe. Not from herself.

He was changing everything. He was rattling her confidence, forcing her to look at the life she'd carved in a new light, and she wasn't sure she liked what she was seeing. She had a job, a home, friends, but none of them were close. She wouldn't let them be.

Rebuffing advances of those who would or could care, she'd encased herself in an emotional jail cell. She was on the inside looking out. She was alone when she didn't have to be, and he was making her wonder why. Yet she knew the answer. She didn't want to be hurt again. She didn't want to risk being controlled again. Not by feelings or by another person.

Deprived of a steady place to live, a steady friend to rely on, and the ability to belong as a girl, she now possessed the security of house and acquaintances and a place in the world. Yet, having fought hard to establish each, she was beginning to realize they meant little if they couldn't be shared, but sharing meant gambling. It meant taking a chance and trusting someone, letting them inside her life and heart, and she didn't know if she was ready. She didn't know if she ever would be, but it already seemed too late to stop it from happening.

He had already edged his way into her world. He knew her better, understood more about her than anyone else, including her own parents. Wherever they were. And she didn't know if she could kick him out.

She wanted to. She was afraid not to. He was strong, perhaps stronger than she, but he didn't abuse his power. At least he hadn't yet. But would he? Given the opportunity? And even if he didn't, if she dared to care, would he stay? Or after she gave all she had to give, would he walk away? Leave her lonelier than before?

Grabbing Arthur to hug the cat close, she hung on as he purred, and she prayed.

She couldn't be falling in love. Not with David. He wasn't her type, he wasn't what she wanted or needed. He just made her feel alive, and she had to decide how much that feeling was worth.

She could go with it, enjoy the moment and deal with the consequences later. Or, she could try to avoid what could happen and never again feel the thrill she did when he held her in his arms.

Chapter 9

CHRISTINE KEPT herself busy the next morning. Taking a taxi to the office, she quickly left again to head to the courthouse to find the talkative clerk she usually took great efforts to avoid.

The woman was efficient, but she could also keep an unwary attorney locked at her counter by the hour. Or anyone else for that matter.

Christine didn't know how or why, but if anything happened in the courthouse, to a lawyer or judge, to anybody who worked in the building, Betty Pitts knew about it. And the pudgy and reliable clerk would share the information with anyone who was brave enough to ask—or happened to be in her sights when the latest piece of gossip just couldn't be kept locked behind her lips any longer.

Yet ready and willing, for once, to be waylaid by the short and slightly overweight woman who had to be forty if a day and who was also a grandmother judging by the pictures on her desk, Christine couldn't get to her. Not until she'd waited in line for half an hour and even shuffled a bit to insure she got Betty instead of one of the other efficiently hustling clerks when she finally reached the counter.

"Good morning, Miss Dunn. How are you today?"

Uncertain where, or how, to begin, Christine smiled. "I'm fine, Betty. Thank you. How are you?"

"Couldn't be better," the woman responded and, uncharacteristically, didn't launch into any type of elaboration that could lead to other things.

Disappointed, Christine quickly set her briefcase on the white formica counter and fumbled for an excuse. "I wonder if you could help me find a case. I seem to have lost the docket number."

Betty smiled and reached out to pat Christine's hand sympathetically. "Of course, I will." She leaned closer. "You know, you work too hard. Everyone says so."

Christine's smile faltered. "Everyone?"

"Everyone who knows you," Betty assured her, resting her forearms on the counter. "They say you're a very good attorney, but rumor is that you never take any time off to have fun."

Suddenly wondering if the man with the briefcase had called on

Betty for information, too, Christine swallowed discomfort and accepted her fate as being part of Betty's rippling pool of knowledge. "Maybe soon," she offered. "Business is picking up now."

"I'm glad for you," Betty said. "Now what's the case you're after?"

Giving her the names involved in a lawsuit she was well acquainted with and whose docket number was in her files, Christine waited while Betty turned to the computer terminal on the other side of the battered and ink stained counter to tap in the information.

"Here it is," Betty told her, seconds later and patiently repeated the number while Christine wrote it on her legal pad. "Is there anything else I can help you with?"

Glancing around to make sure no one was listening, Christine pushed the briefcase out of the way to get close enough to whisper. "I do have a question. If you have a minute."

Sensing conspiracy and grist for the mill, Betty honed in like a homing pigeon and leaned as far over the counter as her five foot four frame would allow. "About what?"

"I don't like to listen to gossip about others," Christine explained.

"Of course not."

"But you've worked here for quite a while..."

"Twenty years."

"That long?" Christine declared with honest surprise.

Betty nodded. "I've seen a lot of people come and go."

"Then you must know Mark Sherman."

Betty's eyes widened. "You're not interested in him are you?"

Christine stammered. "You mean personally? No, I just ...well, I've heard some things."

Betty's sigh was heartfelt. "Well, thank goodness. A nice girl like you doesn't want to get involved with him."

"Why not?"

Betty's lips pursed in disapproval. "It's not for me to say, of course, but it's the general opinion that he hangs out with people you and I wouldn't care to associate with."

"So it's true."

"What?" Betty asked, looking for facts.

"What they say about his clients."

"Bums, all of them," Betty confirmed and glanced down the counter to where other attorneys and clerks were talking. "They say Mr. Sherman will do whatever it takes to get his clients off. Pulls all sorts of sneaky legal maneuvers."

"You mean he bends the law?" Christine encouraged with appropriate horror.

"All but breaks it himself," Betty agreed.

"I hadn't realized," Christine murmured, and she hadn't. Not totally. She wasn't one to listen to rumors or give credence to them without proof, but those about Sherman had been repeated often enough and come to her from enough different sources that she'd been forced to give some merit to the claims even before hearing of his confrontation with Judge Wilson.

Betty nodded sagely.

"I don't suppose you know who his clients are?" Christine asked, hoping for more detail, and when Betty blinked, "Not to be nosey, you understand, but having an office alone, I'd hate to have one of them walk in and not know it."

"You have a good head on your shoulders," Betty assured her. "I wouldn't worry."

Christine sighed and, slipping the legal pad she'd written the case citation on back into her briefcase, snapped it shut again. "I hope so, but it's so hard to tell now days. Even the criminals are wearing business suits."

Betty murmured uncertainly.

Christine heaved the attaché off the counter with a discouraged shrug. "Thanks for the help, Betty," she smiled and knew Betty was thinking about it—giving her a list of names and cases Sherman handled. It was, after all, what Christine was after. "I'll see you around." She turned to go.

"Wait!"

Only two steps away, Christine swallowed her grin and returned to the counter to meet Betty's dark gaze.

"Give me a minute," the older woman whispered. "I'll get you a printout. After you see a few names and addresses, you'll know what I mean."

Betty hustled away, and Christine struggled to hide smug satisfaction. David was going to be very proud of her, and that thought carried her up the stairs and back out to the street where, pushing out the door, she nearly ran straight into Judge Wilson.

"Christine," he greeted with a smile that didn't quite hide the strain he was under. The lines of his face were deeper than before and the shadows under his eyes darker.

"Judge Wilson, how are you?"

He shrugged, looking tired and older than she'd ever seen him.

"I've heard nothing more."

Her fingers closed around his arm in unspoken sympathy. "Don't give up. We're still working on it."

Unexpected moisture clouded his eyes. "I've never felt more helpless. Or angry. It makes me understand vigilantism and the desire for revenge."

"If we take the law into our own hands, we become as lawless as those who refuse to obey the laws made for the betterment of all," she reminded him. And when he stared at her, "A wise man told me that once when I dared to suggest vigilantism had its place in society."

His laugh erased some of the pain from his expression. "That's the trouble with teaching classes, someone's always quoting your words back at you."

"Good words," she told him softly and released his arm. "Don't give up hope."

"I'll never be able to repay you."

"Oh, I don't know," she disagreed with a coy smile. "I could always send you a bill."

Laughing, the man she'd always admired turned away toward the building and his chambers, but she watched him go with a heavy heart. He was hurting. Afraid. And she still didn't know how to help him. Yet the desire reminded her of the list in her briefcase, the one Betty had just given her, and she swung down the steps with a determined stride. At least she had some place to start.

Still looking and knowing what to look for were two different things. Once back in her office, staring at the list of names and cases, she realized none of it really made any sense to her. The people Sherman represented were as unknown to her as he was. More so.

"Why so glum?"

The question had her head jerking up and her heart rate accelerating. David was back, standing in her office door, and he looked none the worse for his encounter in the alley.

His lip was still split, but the swelling was minimal. And the slash on his arm was hidden beneath a charcoal gray suit coat and green polo shirt. At worst his injuries could lead someone to think he had walked into a door. At best he could still make her senses swirl, bruises or not.

"I have a list from the courthouse," she said, holding it up as he shoved the door closed, and suddenly alone with him, she had to take a deep breath to try to steady her pulse.

He frowned and moved forward to take it from her, but if she expected him to be pleased, she was disappointed. "Looks like the same names I got off the department's computer."

"I thought..."

"They have to get arrested first, Chris, before they get put on the court docket."

Disappointed, discouraged she hadn't found something useful after all, she sighed and propped her elbow on the desk and her chin in her hand. "I hadn't thought of that."

He grunted. "Nothing else at the courthouse?"

"No, but I didn't really know what to ask," she apologized and wished she had more to offer. "The only thing I was able to confirm was what I'd already heard—that his clients aren't from the more elite of society."

"Thieves, a couple murderers, but mostly small time thugs," David agreed. "Drugs, prostitution. Basically his job is to keep them out of jail and on the streets. He's pretty good at it."

"Disgusting."

"Fact. Half the legal system tries to put the criminals away, the other half tries to get them out."

"The police versus the lawyers," she murmured. "Except for the prosecutors."

"And attorneys who give a damn about more than a buck," he told her, handing the list back. "Like you."

Her gaze locked with his. "Flattery?"

"What'll it get me?"

She ignored the warning lights blinking in her head and smiled. "What would you like?"

He started to lean across the desk and she moved to meet him halfway, but they never connected. Not before Candy burst through the door with papers in hand.

"Here's that ..," she was saying but stammered to a halt as her abrupt entry forced David and Christine to jerk apart. Her eyes widened at the motion. A desk was separating her two bosses but not by much. Speculation lit her gaze, and she cleared her throat as she beat a hasty retreat. "Sorry."

The door closed behind her, and Christine felt heat rush up her neck to fill her face. In the office she'd always tried to conduct herself like a professional, but at the moment she felt more like a teenager caught necking. Yet it was difficult to regret her *faux pax* even if her secretary's sudden entrance reminded her there was work to be done. "I don't suppose you found out anything?"

Rubbing an ear that she swore was as red as hers, he shook his head. "No, the license plates brought us nothing of value. The red pickup was stolen, and the van belongs to a crook named Buddy Taylor. His record is limited to breaking and entering. No assault or kidnapping. The address is a restaurant with no known links to crime, but I haven't been able to check all of my sources yet. That'll take time."

"We don't have a lot of that," she murmured and rose to walk around the desk to stand beside him. "I saw the judge at the courthouse this morning. I ran into him going into the building."

"Has he been contacted again?"

"No," she denied, shaking her head. "But he looks terrible."

David frowned. "We're doing everything we can, Chris."

"It doesn't seem like enough."

"It never does." He shoved his hands in his pants pockets. "We could call in the FBI. Kidnapping's their jurisdiction."

Her gaze jumped to his. "Would it help?"

He shrugged. "More men, more hands, more eyes and ears."

"Too many?" The more people who were involved, the higher the risk that someone would say the wrong thing to the wrong person, and whoever was holding the judge's son would find out about the investigation.

"We're taking a chance either way. By ourselves or with more help."

She nodded, crossing her arms across her breasts to stop herself from reaching for him. She needed reassurance, but he couldn't give it. Nobody could. When it came to kidnapping, there were no guarantees. "What do we do now?"

"You keep on working," he told her. "So do I."

She stared at him, and her heart skipped when she realized what he was saying. He was going some place she couldn't. Like the alley. "I can't come this time."

"No."

She licked dry lips. "Will you check in?"

"If I can, if I find anything, but it's liable to be a long night."

And he'd be alone mixing with thugs and thieves while trying to find one frightened young man. The taste of fear fouled her mouth. "And tomorrow's Saturday."

"I'll call."

She nodded, wanting to say more, but she didn't know if he'd want to hear it. "Be careful."

"My middle name." His hand lifted to cup her cheek, and she

rested it against his palm. "Stay out of trouble, counselor."

Her smile was bright. "Bill Zaworski's still in jail. He couldn't make bail."

"What a shame."

His hand dropped, he stepped away, and in seconds, he was gone and she was alone once more—but she didn't want to be. For the first time in years she didn't want to be by herself. She wanted to be with someone else. Him.

Closing her eyes briefly, she shook her head. It really was too late. Not only was he in her life, she was already in love with him. Perhaps she had been for a long time. She just hadn't known it, hadn't allowed herself to suspect it was a possibility.

Men were the enemy. That's what she'd always believed, but she'd been wrong. It was her fear that she needed to be afraid of, not the male sex.

Her dread of being ruled, of never being allowed to be independent, of never finding anyone who she would share the ropes of power with had forced her to avoid relationships and hide, but she didn't want to hide any more. She'd found someone she was willing to partner, but did he want her by his side? Did he want what she did? And if he didn't, then what?

How much did she give? How much would he take? And did it really matter as long as they were together?

If he didn't care as much as she did, what was the worst that could happen? She'd end up with a broken heart, but that seemed a small price to pay for whatever part of himself and whatever amount of time he was prepared to let her have.

DAVID SQUINTED against the haze of smoke in the bar. It was late. Near midnight. And he'd been cruising the streets all day, checking sources, asking questions and coming up empty.

He lifted the beer from the scarred counter in front of him and let his gaze drift over the rowdy Friday night crowd. The tavern he'd settled into wasn't classy. Far from it. And the clientele were basically in jeans or grubs instead of satin and lace. Their manners weren't smooth either. They were rough.

The laughter echoing throughout the crowded room was too loud. The tinny music from the juke box was, too, but no one seemed to mind, including him.

He was tired. Fed up. Frustrated. The harder he tried, the more dead ends he found. Nobody knew anything, or at least nobody was talking. That or he was looking in all of the wrong places. The trouble was he didn't know where else to go and search.

"Mind some company, Maverick?"

Startled that someone would recognize him in a place he never frequented, he spun on the bar stool and smiled when he saw who was waiting. "Griff."

The man called Griffin grinned, showing off a mouthful of white teeth and deep dimples that accented his beach boy blond good looks. The only thing that didn't fit the image was his eyes. Pale blue, David had seen them go nearly white in rage. It was a chilly sight.

"I hear you're causing trouble down this end of town," Griff said, motioning for a beer from the bartender who, broad as he was tall, waddled over to slap a less than spotless glass filled with brew down on the counter.

"Where'd you hear that?" David asked as his friend took the stool beside him.

"Some kid with a sore head," Griff responded, sipping past the white froth to the golden ale. "Said some dame hanging around with a guy with a patch hit him over the head with a garbage can."

David nearly choked on his own drink. "It was the lid."

"And who was the dame?"

"Lady," David corrected and saw interest arch blond eyebrows. Griffin had been a cop, too, but he hadn't been forced out on disability. He'd quit—after the two felons who had shot him and killed his partner had gotten off on a technicality. "How's the bounty hunting?"

"Good. I could use a partner, but don't change the subject."

David grinned and held out his hand, glad to see a friend and appreciating the firm grasp of Griffin's fingers in his. "Long time no see," he murmured. "You look good."

"So do you."

"Thanks to some help from a few friends."

Griff nodded but said nothing. He wouldn't take credit for being the one to help shake David from his hospital bed. He wouldn't admit he knew what it was like to be wounded, too. And scared. "So who is she?"

"My partner."

Griff spit out his drink. "What?"

"An attorney actually."

Griff wiped at the beer he'd splattered. "This is getting better."

"We share office space."

"That all?"

"What do you care?"

Griffin grinned. "Because I know you, buddy."

David shook his head and looked away.

"Still worried about losing that other eye?"

Mention of his deepest fear had David glaring at Griffin.

"And that no woman could get past the patch to the man behind it?"

The barbs hit close, and David chugged some brew to ease the sting. "I don't see anyone hanging on your arm."

"That's because I'm not looking."

"And I am?"

"You were married once," Griff pointed out. "And you liked it."

David nodded. He had. Coming home to something, someone. It was what he'd always wanted. Still did. He just wasn't sure he could have it. "Our jobs don't mix well with matrimony."

Griff grunted. "Yeah? Is that why every bounty hunter on my team is married except me?"

David frowned.

"You're still running, David. Give her a chance. Sounds like she's got some moxie. Not everyone can make their way in an alley."

David snorted. "You weren't there. You should have heard her when she stepped on something that didn't smell good."

"But she didn't faint at the sight of blood."

David cocked an eyebrow. "You heard that, too?"

"Switchblade?"

"It's hers now."

Griff nodded. "What were you two after?"

"A van and a briefcase filled with money."

"Want to tell me about it?"

David did. If anyone knew what was going down in the city, Griff would. If anyone could help him, Griff could.

"Sherman, huh?" Griff asked, his face grim with distaste and dislike. "He represents a good many of the guys I haul in, but if he's involved in kidnapping, he's jumped from the minors to the big league."

"That's what I figured," David agreed. "He's setting his sights kind of high, and I can't imagine who's helping him. None of his marks are into anything that touches on federal beyond dealing drugs."

"Your sources came up with nothing?"

"So far, but it's only been twenty-four hours."

"I can put some feelers out."

"The judge would appreciate it."

Griff scowled. "I don't much care for judges, or attorneys, but I'll help a friend."

David grinned and slapped him on the shoulder. "Still prejudiced, I see."

Griff lifted his glass. "I..."

A body slammed into his with a roar. The impact threw the beer in his glass in all directions, but most of it ended up decorating his face. And the bar. Still Griffin didn't move. He didn't even breathe as the man who'd collided with him stumbled away without apology to go after the one who'd pushed him.

David didn't budge either. He just watched Griff calmly wipe ale from his face as the fight behind them heated up.

"You finding anything of interest here?"

David drew a hand down his own face to clean it of the spattered foam that had caught him, but he wasn't fooled by the cool tone of the question. Something besides ale was brewing. "Nope."

"Then maybe we should leave."

David grinned and shoved his beer aside. He could feel the adrenaline starting to pump as glass and tempers broke a few feet away. "I'm about ready."

Griff stood up. "I get first swing."

"Only if I don't reach that guy first. This is a brand new jacket."

Two more bodies came their way, struggling against each other and the momentum driving their steps, and David and Griff grabbed one each.

"Just like old times," David said and planted his knuckles into a square jaw. His victim reeled backwards, causing shouts and curses when he landed on a table ladened with unfinished drinks.

Griff's sacrifice followed with a similar bang. "Last man standing buys the drinks."

"You're on," David agreed and led the charge into chaos.

THE DOORBELL rang. David could hear it echo for the third time, and he could hear her coming. Mumbling to her cat. He grinned and immediately winced. He'd split his lip again.

A muffled exclamation came from behind the wood, and a chain rattled before the bolt was thrown. In a second she was standing there, staring at him with an open mouth and in a nightgown of creamy satin.

"Got any ice?" he asked, nearly swallowing his tongue at the sight of her. A Popsicle in the summer time was his favorite treat, and he could lick her from end to end.

She grabbed his hand and dragged him inside but recoiled when he got too close. "Is that beer I smell?"

"Mostly on the outside," he assured her.

She slammed the door and grimaced at him. "Your lip is bleeding."

He started to grab the hand she lifted to touch his mouth, but she whirled before he could catch it and headed toward the kitchen. "Go sit down."

"Always giving orders," he muttered but did as he was told instead of following her and the scent of her perfume into the other room. That and the sway of a satin clad backside.

In the den, Arthur the cat was waiting, glaring at him with regal elegance and disapproval. Obviously he wasn't used to late night callers or having his sleep disturbed.

"Hi, Art," David greeted, but his hand was greeted by a hiss and an unfriendly whack before the cat disappeared down the hall. David frowned. "He must not like beer either."

"What did you say?"

He spun to see Christine approaching, ice bag in hand, and had to scramble to keep his legs under him when the room unexpectedly tilted.

"All the beer's on the outside, huh?" she asked, catching his arm and pushing him into a chair.

"Most of it," he repeated and tried to remember how many he'd tossed back with Griff after the fight. He couldn't recall exactly, but at least he hadn't ended up with a black eye. Griff was going to have a real shiner.

"Uh-huh," she agreed and held out a hand. "Give me the jacket, and you can have the ice."

He struggled out of the denim coat that was stained with beer and blood and let her take it away before pressing the ice to his mouth. He swore at the sting.

"You okay?" she asked, returning to kneel beside him.

Her hair was down, glowing in the lamp light as it lay across her shoulders. He reached for it, and she caught his hand.

"What happened?"

"We got in a fight."

"We?"

"Griff and me. We're friends."

She nodded. "He's helping you?"

"He will be now. I met him tonight. He's the best. A bounty hunter, you know."

"No, I didn't," she denied, hiding what he suspiciously thought might be a smile. "Have you known him long?"

"We were cops together," David told her. "He understands. About the eye."

Her smile faded.

"He helped me up when I was down, and he knows how I feel."

"About losing your eye?"

"About maybe losing the other," David clarified, sinking back against the chair. It felt good. He was tired. He'd gotten little sleep over the last seventy-two hours, and now he'd stopped moving, the liquor was making him drowsy. "And about the women."

His arm drooped with fatigue, and she reached out to take the ice from him. "Tell me," she said, sitting on the arm of the chair to hold the cloth she'd wrapped the cubes in to his lip.

"They're like groupies. They chase cops around because they've never had one. It's the uniform or something that attracts them." He shrugged. "But for me, now it's not being a cop. It's the patch. It makes me a different kind of freak."

Her hand brushed the hair from his forehead. "I don't think it makes you a freak. I think it makes you look dashing."

"Dashing?" he frowned. He wasn't sure he liked the word.

"Like a pirate."

Her smile warmed him the way the beer couldn't, and he let his head sag back against the chair to bask in it as he gazed up at her. "A pirate?"

She nodded and continued to stroke his hair. "When you came in the office the other day wearing an earring, I thought the only thing you needed was a kerchief for your head and a sword at your side."

He grunted. "I suppose that means I shouldn't tell you that I don't like boats. They make me sick."

"You can stay on shore then."

"Okay," he agreed on a contented sigh. Her touch was relaxing, the chair soft, and his bones weary. "I'm really tired."

"It's three in the morning, no wonder."

His eye drifted closed. "Would you mind if I rested here for a bit?"

"Not at all."

"I've got to tell you..."

"Later," she told him, and the last thing he remembered before drifting off was her kiss. Brushing her lips against his in the tenderest of caresses, it chased him into the world of dreams.

Chapter 10

DAVID WOKE slowly. And with a crick in his neck.

Grumbling to himself, he straightened the muscles holding his head in place and groaned. It was no wonder his neck hurt. He wasn't sleeping laying down. He was in a chair.

Muttering at his own stupidity, he shifted, tried to pry his eye open and winced when other pains began making themselves known. Ribs, back, head, knuckles. Everything ached. In fact, his whole body felt as if it'd been used as a battering ram, especially his jaw.

Finally managing to look at the world, he raised a hand to rub his throbbing chin bone and stopped. He wasn't in his apartment. He was in Christine's.

A moan rumbled in his throat, and memory returned with a disturbing rush.

He'd been out searching for answers and had ended up in a bar where he'd met and gotten into a fight with Griffin. The combat had felt good at the moment. The pairing, the release of frustration accompanied by a surge of adrenaline, but when it had all been over, his one thought had been for her.

Dragging a hand over his face, he muttered darkly, remembering his drunken need to give her a progress report. Unbelievably, she'd actually let him in to listen.

He sighed disgust. She shouldn't have. She should have told him to get lost. To go home and sleep it off. Instead she'd given him ice for his hurts, an ear for his babble, and her chair for a bed. She'd even given him a good night kiss.

Sitting up straighter, he pushed the afghan she'd thoughtfully covered him with off and swore at his own ridiculous actions that had taken him to her door step. Yet he stilled when he thought about what she'd done.

She could have turned away. She would have had every right to. Not actually drunk, just over tired and filled with and stinking of beer, he'd probably made little if any sense. He shook his head. It was beyond him why she'd taken him in, but he liked that she had. He liked her. And what she'd done made him think maybe Griff was right. Again.

He scowled blackly. It was irritating that his friend was so good at reading people. Better than him, better than he ever hoped to be, Griff's instincts were above question, and Griff thought Christine should be given a chance. And, it appeared, with just cause.

Confronted with a man who was too unsteady to stand and too full of liquor to show good sense, she hadn't rejected him. She hadn't even berated him for his behavior. She'd simply taken him in. Accepted him. Like she always had.

Never could he remember her being repulsed by him or his scars. Not when they first met, not when they became business partners, and not when he came to her bloody and battered. Always she took him as he was—as her business partner, as a private eye, as a man....

Swallowing, he abruptly stood. He didn't want to go where his thoughts were taking him. He wasn't looking for a mate. He wasn't looking for attachments. But she'd kissed him. He might not remember what he'd said to her, but he remembered that. And the embrace offered possibilities he didn't know if he was ready to deal with. Yet suddenly he had to because she was standing in the room with him.

Fresh from the shower, with a towel wrapped around her head and in a pink robe that was damp in spots that told him she wasn't wearing anything underneath, she was watching him. His heart skipped, his blood pooled in his groin, and he tried not to swallow his tongue.

"You're awake."

Her greeting was hesitant, her smile shy and her hands nervous. Like his stomach. He cleared his throat. "I, ah. Yes, I am."

She fidgeted, pulling at the lapels of her robe. The action stretched the material over her breasts and nearly had him groaning out loud.

"I'm sorry," he stammered. "About...crashing here. I shouldn't have come."

"I didn't mind."

And she didn't. He could see it in her eyes. Warm blue orbs that had him stepping forward when he should have been running away. "I could have waited until this morning to call."

"It was morning when you arrived."

Her lips twitched in amusement, and uncomfortable heat crept up his neck. "Yeah, well, I should probably go." But he was standing in front of her, and he didn't want to leave.

She moved slightly, halving the short distance separating them. "You don't have to. Besides, you haven't told me why you stopped in the first place. You must have had something important to say."

"I did," he agreed, noting some hair had slipped free of the restraining towel. He reached out to tuck it back inside but ended up tracing the line of her jaw instead.

"What was it?"

"I can't remember."

And he couldn't. His memory was abruptly gone. Everything he knew was forgotten. Nothing made sense any more. Except her. She was the only thing that was real, the only thing that mattered, and when he reached for her, she slid silently into his arms. And why not?

It was, after all, where she wanted to be. Against him with his mouth devouring hers. She could taste his desperation. It matched her own.

She needed him. Now. Forever. How ever long he'd have her, and her unconditional surrender made his hands shake and his blood burn hot.

A tug had the towel around her head dropping unnoticed to the floor, and he immediately plunged his hands into her hair that was damp and dark and thick enough to tangle his fingers in. He used the tresses to angle her head and her lips for a more effective frontal assault.

He wanted, needed, to possess her, and the tentative touch of her palms sliding over his back, the press of her breasts against his chest, the line of her legs against his urged him to take what he wanted to have. She was setting him on fire, but his wish wasn't to consume. And he didn't want to be the only one lost in the flames. She was going into the inferno with him.

Raising his head, he smiled down at her, and the predatory gleam in his gaze made her pulse flutter.

"What?" she asked, barely able to speak and hanging on when he unexpectedly started walking. Backwards. With her.

"You just had a shower."

She nodded, unable to look away, trapped like a butterfly by the flicker of a candle's blaze.

"I need one, too."

The suggestion was erotic, the hunger in his stare arousing, and she licked her lips in anticipation. "The bathroom's this way."

His smile widened. "I know."

A second later they stepped inside together. Legs brushing, hands clinging, hearts pounding. She trembled when he closed the door.

The room was small, hot and filled with steam that had been

dissipating, but it began to rise again when he leaned away to twist the shower faucet on.

"I'd like you to rub my back."

The demand was brazen—just like she wanted to be. She reached for and tugged on the tee shirt tucked into his black jeans. "You have to get undressed first."

He helped her toss the offending garment aside, ready and willing to assist her disrobe, too, but she stopped him—with a touch.

She liked the hiss of pleasure that escaped his lips when she dragged her hands up his rib cage with exploratory wonder. Beneath her palms, his skin was hot, the muscles hard and the spattering of dark hair covering his chest soft. The contradictions appealed—and were magnified when her fingers skimmed over his collar bone before brushing the stubble lining his jaw.

She wrinkled her nose. "You need a shave, too."

"Got a razor?" he asked, reaching for the belt securing the robe to her waist.

"No, I like you just the way you are."

He grinned and dipped his head to hers to find her waiting. And eager. But no more than he. The sash came loose, the robe separated and he slid his hands inside.

She gasped when calloused skin met smooth flesh, and he greedily pulled her closer as he searched curves, caressed bends and massaged her derriere that was firm and soft before cupping breasts that fit in his hands with perfect symmetry.

Diving down to taste her neck, nibble her throat and nip her ear lobe, he growled when she pulled free enough to grapple for his belt and the zipper of his jeans.

A few tugs and denim slid free at the same time he pushed the silk from her shoulders. Both garments pooled at their feet, and he rapidly toed out of shoes, socks and underwear before swinging her up into his arms.

"Time to get wet," he murmured and carried her into the spray.

Hot, the water stung. She squealed a protest and he released her to fumble for the knob, but while he tried to adjust the temperature of the shower, she grabbed for the soap and slipped behind him.

His back was a plane of ridges and rippling power. Ligaments, tendons and muscles wove and flexed together in an awesome display of hidden strength that tapered to a waist that was slim and buttocks that were hard. Yet she wasn't allowed to scrub or gaze for long. He quickly spun to snatch the suds giving bar from her.

She gasped when he slid it over her stomach, but in the confined space, escape wasn't an option. Even if she wanted to, and she didn't. Not from him. She wanted to stay instead, and he was ready to lead her through the dance of tease and torment.

Fingers massaged soft flesh, hands explored hard planes, and water splashed unnoticed onto walls and shower doors as legs and tongues tangled.

Yet, eventually, touching wasn't enough. He killed the flow of spray, stepped from the tub and the miniature tempest swirling toward the drain, and pulled her with him out of the shower and onto the waiting bath mat.

Automatically she reached for a towel, but he grabbed for the door knob. He liked her slick and wet and dripping, and he steered her into the hall in quest of the bedroom. What he found was the closet.

Laughing at his discovery, her flesh sliding off of his, she spun away toward another door, and he hastily followed, tackling her when she was close to the bed.

She screamed as they hit, bounced, and startled her cat from where it'd been sleeping on the pillow. "We scared Arthur."

"He hasn't seen anything yet," David assured her, and she rolled with him into a tangle of limbs as old as time.

Together they began the exploration again. Murmuring, stroking, each sought ways to please the other as they stumbled up the steps of discovery.

Eventually his hands found her thighs, and hers fingers clasped his shoulders to draw him closer as she opened herself to let him inside. They merged on a sigh.

With arms braced on either side of her, he bent to capture her lips with his. The tenderness of the embrace brought tears to her eyes, but she didn't let him see. Instead she wrapped her arms around him and held him close as his hips began to move with hers.

The gentle pace stirred more primal forces, and soon the drive for release accelerated the speed of copulation from soothing to frantic.

They rode the tide together, straining, groping, reaching as one until they hit the crest on a cry.

Euphoria doused the burning embers of passion, and they collapsed to lay breathless in an unmoving heap. Sated, satisfied, stunned and with hearts racing double time, limbs and bodies remained entwined in the quiet pool of aftermath.

Buried beneath him, she absorbed his weight with more ease than she would have believed possible. Yet if she was willing, he wasn't ready to allow her to take the burden. He shifted away, but he didn't leave her side. Or her. His fingers found and tangled with hers, and she closed her eyes to again hide the depth of meaning the gesture had for her.

Never had she felt closer to anyone. Never had she felt more complete when with a man. Absent was the sense of domination. The need to please didn't exist. It was replaced by desire and the spirit of belonging.

"Counselor, have you ever thought about going into corporate law?"

Frowning at the murmured question, she turned her head to look at him in surprise. "No, why?"

"You're a real expert on merging."

His grin was silly and his compliment invigorating. She rolled to one elbow to run a hand over his chest. Beneath her palm, she could still feel the racing of his heart. "You should see me on hostile takeovers."

He reached up to bring her head down to his. "I can't wait."

The kiss was long and draining, and she collapsed to lay against him with a heartfelt sigh. His arm automatically circled around to scoop and hold her close, and she nuzzled into his shoulder. "You know, as a private investigator, I've been meaning to tell you. You've got good instincts—and great moves."

"Yeah?" he asked, turning his head on the pillow to meet her gaze. "Wait until you see me undercover."

The sheet from the yet as unmade bed was abruptly flipped up and over both of them, and she squealed as he attacked her with a whisker rub before expertly flipping her so that she lay on top of him with the sheet tented over her.

"You're crazy," she said, smiling down at him.

"One of my more redeeming qualities, don't you think?" he asked, settling her hips over his. The motion testified to his growing readiness to impress her again, but she was in no hurry.

Savoring the unexpected feeling of power, hers to stir him, she leaned closer to use her tongue to trace the outline of his lips while burying her fingers in the thick, darkness of his hair.

His hands immediately settled on her waist. "Counselor, if you're prepared to present your next case, I do believe I'm prepared to prosecute."

"What about preliminary motions?" she asked and allowed her breasts to lightly graze his chest. The quick inhalation of his breath said he got her point.

"What'd you have in mind?" he asked.

She stroked his hair away from his forehead. "Maybe some discovery is in order."

"As long as I don't need my briefs."

Still holding his head in place, she followed the line of his jaw, rough with stubble, with her lips. "They won't be necessary."

"Good," he said, shifting beneath her, but he suddenly stilled when the fingers in his hair found the string that circled his head to hold the patch in place.

Aware of the change, of his sensitivity to an old wound that was still raw, she quickly pressed her mouth to his in silent reassurance. "Do you ever take this off?"

"Not in public."

"We're not in public," she whispered, but his hand was harsh when it grabbed hers to stop it from removing the patch from his eye. Yet determined to show him that what he saw as a handicap was nothing to her, she met his fearful gaze with an arched brow. "Mr. Maverick, don't you know that what you have left over is more than most men start out with?"

He blinked, she pulled the patch free, and tossing it aside, with infinite care, she kissed the scar that continued to cause him pain.

"Christine..."

She quickly put a finger to stop his words. "Don't tell me. Show me."

And he did. Carefully, slowly and with unlimited patience, his hands, his mouth, his body explained how much her acceptance meant, and she was devastated by his tenderness, brutalized by his gentleness and terrified he might realize the truth. She didn't merely accept him as he was. She loved him to the depths of her soul.

DAVID HUNG up the phone with a frustrated sigh.

"Nothing?"

The word startled him, and he looked up to find Christine standing silently nearby. Back in her silken robe, she was watching him from the hall—just as she had been many hours before....

Before the shower, before the lovemaking that had left him exhausted and nearly witless, and before sleep and intimate sharing the like of which he'd never experienced. His pulse quickened on memory and because of her.

Outside and beyond the windows, the sun was setting, but he'd never seen it rise and never noticed when it'd crossed its zenith. He'd only been aware of her.

All the passion she used to attack her cases, to defend her clients, to right wrongs she'd given to him. Freely. Completely. It scared the hell out of him.

She moved him like no woman ever had. He felt her touch all the way down to the bone, and her understanding surpassed his own. At least when it came to him. To scars and pain he didn't need to speak of for her to comprehend.

She made him want to make declarations better left unsaid, to promise things he couldn't give. Like commitment. Yet she hadn't asked for any, and in her eyes he could see no plea for one. That made him feel guilty. And it made him want her all the more.

To her, he wanted to give forever. Like a lovesick fool, his desire spurred him to forget what he did, who he was, how he lived and what his future held. A career of carrying a gun, taking risks, confronting danger, running along the edge of the law like Griffin because he wanted to help enforce it in ways those in uniform could not.

Hampered by statutes and policies and legalisms that tied hands, set criminals free and barred attempts to search and seize, private detectives and bounty hunters didn't have to confine their actions to those allowed by the strict letter of the law. They could bend it, break it and get away with it. And risk everything in the process.

His wife had left him because of the fear enforcing the rights of others generated, and that had been during the time when he wasn't working along the fine line of right and wrong. The worry would be greater without a uniform, without a force of others at his side, and he couldn't—wouldn't—subject anyone else to that strain, that stress, even if she could accept him and his scars.

The patch was back on, but he didn't feel he needed it any more. Not with her. She'd seen and dealt with his pain, both inside and out, and standing to face her, shirtless and shoeless, he wanted to give her everything he could in return. Everything that was for her own good. And that wasn't him.

"Nothing," he confirmed and sighed again. "But I haven't been able to reach Griff yet."

She moved closer. "You mentioned him last night."

"He's a friend."

"You mentioned that, too," she agreed and cocked her head. "Did he go home stinking of beer, too?"

David grinned. "He went home with a black eye."

She lifted a brow in query. "You didn't give it to him?"

"No, otherwise I'd have one, too."

Both eyebrows went up. "I think I'd like to meet him."

"He's a bounty hunter."

She shrugged, apparently unimpressed by his warning tone. "That's what you want to be."

"It goes with being a private eye."

"Dark alleys, fist fights." She shook her head and brushed at the hair that remained in loose disarray around her shoulders. "Such a life."

"It's dangerous," he agreed, trying to make her understand his daily reality.

"So's being an attorney," she said and stifled a yawn. "Remember Bill Zaworski?"

David scowled, the comment jogging more than memory.

"I put the rest of your clothes in the wash," she said, stepping closer. "If you want to give me your pants, I can throw them in, too."

His teeth flashed before he could stop it. "But whatever will I do without clothes to wear?"

She avoided his questing grasp and his question. "Are you hungry?"

"I could eat," he agreed, following her as she retreated toward the kitchen.

"Food," she corrected, noting his leer.

"That, too."

She laughed and held out her hand. "I think we'll get something in your stomach before we worry about washing your pants."

"Eating will give me more energy," he said, capturing her fingers with his.

She frowned. "Maybe we should go back to bed then."

"Naw, I wouldn't want to disappoint you," he denied, stopping her mock attempt to escape out the door and get away from him. He put a hand over his abdomen, and his forehead came to rest against hers. "I'm running on empty."

"When did you last eat?"

"Food?" he asked and earned a well-aimed glare that had his hands raising in self-defense. "I'm not sure. Yesterday some time."

She rolled her eyes and left him for the refrigerator. "Men."

"What?" he asked, ready to defend his sex. "We have more important things to think about than our stomachs."

"Like saving the world?"

"Like rescuing damsels in distress," he corrected and padded across the room to watch her throw eggs and bacon into some pans. "Breakfast?"

"Objections?"

"It's going on six. At night."

"But we just got out of bed."

"So we did," he confirmed on a sigh and placed a kiss on the back of her neck. Still, exposing the tender skin there, he winced when he noted a red mark on the otherwise white flesh. One he'd caused. Lifting a hand, he rubbed his whisker lined jaw. "Maybe I should shave."

She eyed him over her shoulder as the bacon started to sizzle. "You can use mine, but I have to warn you, it's made for women."

"And legs." He glanced down to admire hers through the slit in the robe. "It wouldn't be the first time."

"Your wife?"

"Hmmm," he agreed, reluctant to leave her—and the smell of the meal she was creating—but he was willing to make the sacrifice in hopes of dessert while his pants were being cleaned.

"Have you been divorced long?"

"Three years," he confessed, pausing on his way to the door. "The stress was too much for her."

"Being married to a cop?"

He nodded. "Never knowing where I was, always wondering if she'd get that call."

"It wouldn't be easy for everyone."

"You mean anyone," he corrected.

"No, I mean everyone," she denied mildly, grabbing some cheese from the refrigerator to add to the omelet forming in the pan. "Some women could take it. Others never would be able to. Just like some men can be cops and some can't. It's human nature."

Scowling, he met her eye doubtfully.

"Some of the cops you know are married, right?" she asked, sensing his disagreement with her opinion.

"Yeah."

"And some of them have been married for a long time, true?"

"True," he admitted and watched her shrug.

"I rest my case."

She turned back to the stove, and he drifted out the door to the bathroom and the razor. But he was thinking. Again. About her. And about possibilities.

Chapter 11

"WHAT ARE you going to do?" Christine asked, watching David pull on his washed and dried denim jacket. It'd been on a hanger all night. And throughout the next day. Saturday was gone, and Sunday was rapidly passing. The sun was getting ready to set again, and he was leaving. She tried not to tremble at the sudden chill his departure brought to her heart.

"Talk to some people. Meet Griff. He thinks he may have a lead."

She nodded, feeling cold in the robe she hadn't gotten far away from all weekend. She'd greeted him in it at the door early Saturday morning and had been in and out of it ever since, and that was unusual. She wasn't one to lounge around over the weekend and not get dressed, but she didn't usually have a man in bed with her for forty-eight hours either. "We only have a couple more days."

"And we're going to make the most of them, believe me."

"I do," she acknowledged, her confidence in him unwavering as he turned to face her.

"We won't give up."

"No, we won't."

His expression darkened. "But it's beginning to look like you're going to have to go ahead with that meeting with Sherman tomorrow."

The idea didn't please him. She could tell. It didn't particularly please her either. She smothered a sigh, not dreading the coming confrontation but not looking forward to it either. It was just something that had to be done. "He'll be there at nine o'clock."

"Remember," David cautioned. "If you don't see me when you get there or before he arrives..."

"It doesn't mean you're not there," she interrupted. "It just means you're out of sight."

"Exactly," he agreed, and she bit her lip.

They'd already been over the plan. David would stay unseen and unheard in his office while she met with Sherman alone in hers, but if he wasn't present for the meeting, that didn't mean David wouldn't be listening.

Before Sherman arrived, before she arrived, he would be in her office setting up equipment that would allow him to tape whatever was said and hear every word as it was spoken. If anything went wrong, he could be with her in a matter of seconds, but that wasn't what worried her.

She shook her head. "I just wish ..."

He stepped forward to slip his arms around her and to offer understanding. "It'll be over soon, and we'll find him in time."

Unable to speak, she clung instead. In the city somewhere there was a young man. Barely twenty years old, he was supposed to have his life in front of him, but instead it was in the hands of those ready to kill to get their way. "He must be terrified."

"No more than us. Or his father."

Comforted by the strength of his arms around her, she raised her head. "Will you call me?"

"Only if I have any news."

She stepped away, relieved that at least he wouldn't be going into the unknown alone. His friend, Griffin, would be with him. "You won't come back tonight?"

"Is that an invitation?"

His cheeky grin made her laugh. "As long as you don't bring any beer."

"Deal," he agreed and leaned forward to press a kiss to her forehead. "Get some rest."

"Me and Arthur," she agreed and scooped up the cat. Arthur had been swept into the background for most of the weekend, but her pet had been bold enough to demand attention when he'd wanted it—and when the romps in bed had stilled long enough to allow him the chance to make his presence known.

"Replaced by another male already," David complained but reached out to scratch the purring feline's ears anyway.

"He likes you," she commented, recognizing and accepting the male bonding that had already been cemented by their sharing of her.

"I like him, too, but I like his owner better." David's hand dropped. "I have to go."

Clutching the cat to stop herself from asking him to stay, to selfishly keep him with her while she could instead of letting him leave to do what needed to be done, she followed him to the entrance hall. "Be careful. I'll be here hoping for a call."

"And I'll talk to you in the morning if not before."

He opened the door, and she held her breath—and he abruptly stole it by unexpectedly swinging back to grab her by the neck to crush her lips with his.

"I'll have to take a continuance for now, counselor," he growled in a hoarse whisper. "But I'm looking forward to our next hearing."

Heart fluttering, she forced a smile. "Maybe I'll let you present your briefs."

Nose-to-nose with her, she could almost taste his smile. "And you can show me your motion for new trial."

She opened her mouth to retort, but the door closed and he was gone. She hugged Arthur. "He's not bad for a man, don't you think?"

The response was somewhere between a meow and a purr and totally indecipherable to human ears, but at least she wasn't alone. Not totally.

Twisting the locks into place, she slowly moved back into the living room that suddenly seemed very empty and very still without someone else in it with her. Him. But she didn't let herself think about that. She didn't let herself think or wonder or worry because it was counter productive and because she wasn't ready to let fear control her life. She also had faith in him and his abilities.

He wasn't reckless. He wouldn't take any unnecessary chances, and he had a friend. Someone who would be working with him, who would search as he was, to find an answer to the riddle of Mark Sherman and Jimmy Wilson.

All of those factors combined made it easy for her to turn her energy to the tasks usually completed by Sunday afternoon. Laundry, dishes, some touch up ironing. The mundane and normal didn't totally erase the worry. Chores didn't and couldn't prevent the concern that they might lose the race against time, but by being able to keep busy through the rest of the evening hours, when she crawled into bed hours later on clean sheets that didn't carry his scent, she was tired enough to drift into dreams without having to first fight off any demons.

Not about him and his safety or about how they would ever unravel the mystery of a briefcase and a kidnapping and not about them. She accepted that he was hers for the moment and that the future couldn't matter. Not when the present made her so happy.

RISING THE next day, she took great care with choosing what to wear and how she styled her hair. Not because she wanted to impress David but because she was meeting an enemy.

Faith in the professionalism of her appearance would bolster her confidence during the confrontation. She just wished the clothes she had on would do something to settle her nerves.

Already starting to stir when she locked her condominium's door, the flutter of butterflies in her stomach only got worse when she climbed into her car in the underground garage and left the building to join others in the Monday morning rush for job, office and paycheck.

The drive proved to be an uphill battle. Traffic was snarled, drivers irritable and impatient, and timing critical. Yet she barely made it to the office before Mark Sherman arrived. He stepped through the door mere minutes after she did and caught her still holding her briefcase and standing in front of Mandy's desk.

"Christine."

His greeting was warm and given with a smile that seemed sincere enough, but it was difficult for her to duplicate his cordiality. He was a kidnapper, or at the very least, a conspirator in a kidnapping. And he was blackmailing a judge, an officer of the court.

Yet searching his face that was thin and long beneath hair that was dark and slicked back from a high brow, it was hard to tell he was less law abiding than any other person, or attorney, she'd ever met.

Forcing her lips to curve into an appropriate expression of welcome, she nodded. "Mark."

He extended a hand, an attaché in his other. "I see you're just arriving. Am I too early?"

"No," she denied, accepting his fingers in hers with brief ceremony before motioning him toward her office. "Not at all. I just got caught in traffic."

"It's bad today," he sympathized and followed her as she led him past Mandy to her open office door. "You're lucky you don't have to fight it every time you want to go to the courthouse."

"Part of my plan," she assured him and paused to reach inside to flick on the lights. A swift survey of the room gave no indication of David's presence in the room earlier that morning, but she was certain he had been inside—just as she was sure he was behind the closed door of the office on the other side of the suite. She couldn't see him, but he was with her.

Still, setting her briefcase down before moving to her chair, she wished she could have talked to him, however briefly, before meeting Sherman, and she would have preferred to have some time after arriving in the office to gather her wits before proceeding with the confrontation. Unfortunately, she couldn't do either. Her adversary was already with her. No more delays were possible. Or necessary. She was ready.

"Would you like some coffee?" she asked, playing polite hostess when she would have preferred the role of prosecutor. She had questions she wanted to ask, but they would have to wait for the proper opening.

Sherman grimaced, unbuttoning his suit coat which was tan and tailored to perfection before taking a seat opposite her desk. "I could use some caffeine if you have it available."

Glad her hand wasn't shaking when she reached for the intercom, she buzzed the twins. The need to cater to the man's wants galled. She didn't want to serve him or have the twins act as waitresses on his behalf, but it was a necessity and a routine agreed to by Candy and Mandy. Guests got served. Bosses served themselves. "Mandy, I'm sorry to interrupt, but would you mind bringing Mr. Sherman some coffee?"

"Not at all," came the quick reply, and Christine slipped on to her chair and spent the next few minutes caught up in grueling small talk and chit chat. The strain of idle conversation had her clenching her hands together on top of the desk, but once the steaming cups of brew were handed out and Mandy disappeared back out the door, the fencing she was expecting and looking forward to began.

"An acquaintance of mine asked me to come to see you," Sherman began, sipping his coffee with casual ease.

"Anyone I know?"

"Just a man with a briefcase."

The unexpected and abrupt reference to the leather attaché filled with money took her aback and left her struggling to determine how best to react. What would Sherman expect?

"I know all about it," he said when she hesitated. "How you found it at the courthouse, the exchange you made on the street and, of course, the fee you accepted in return for giving the briefcase back."

Not looking away from his gaze that was both dark and unreadable, deciding it was best to let him do the talking, she moved her shoulders noncommittally. "You have me at a disadvantage."

"I'm sure," he agreed, but his teeth flashed in quick reassurance. "But you've nothing to worry about from me. I understand exactly what you're going through."

"You do?" she asked, wondering where the conversation was going—and where he wanted to take her.

His gesture encompassed her office. "We're both single practitioners. If you don't work, the bills don't get paid. Sometimes they don't get paid even when you do work because one of the people who hires you refuses to send in a check."

Her eyes dropped from his in a motion he would see as

acquiescence, but it was really to hide the denial she wanted to give. Since beginning her practice, she'd been fortunate. None of her clients had ever failed to pay her bill. Some had been slow to pay, some had needed to pay over a few months' time, but she hadn't been stiffed yet, even though she knew attorneys who had become victims of the dollar, of clients who were unable or unwilling to pay for services rendered.

"How would you like to be guaranteed that wouldn't ever happen again?" he asked, sitting forward on the edge of the chair. "How would you like to know that every time a client walks through your door, you won't have to worry about the bottom line? Or the rent?"

She sat forward, too. "That's impossible."

"Is it?" He shrugged and stood to set his coffee cup on the desk. "Most of my clients have bosses who keep me on retainer. They pay me to be available in the event one of their employees might happen to have some trouble with the law. That means I never have to worry about my fee. Not only am I paid in advance just to be ready to act should the need arise, I know I'll also be paid for any time or additional costs incurred in looking after any employee's best interests. Guaranteed."

She cocked her head, forced to admire his play with words. No admissions, no confessions, nothing that could be used against him. He was just talking business, but she wanted more and decided to take a chance. "I've heard about some of your clientele."

"Have you?" he asked. "They're nice people. I think you'd like them. I do because they always pay their bills on time as long I do my job."

"Which is?"

He held his hands out in a gesture of innocence. "I act as their attorney. I represent them in court, and I remember that my main goal is to keep their employees out of jail and out of trouble."

She sat back in her chair to study him. "But why tell me?"

"I'm offering a referral. If you're interested."

She wasn't. Not really, but she had to pretend to be. She just wasn't sure how eager she should appear to be, or how coy.

"This can be the only meeting we have," Sherman offered when she didn't speak immediately. "Or we can have another."

Her heart skipped at the sudden opportunity. "With a potential client?"

"With someone who's interested in your work and who's impressed by your cool," Sherman agreed, strolling to the window to look outside. "He doesn't like people who panic. Or who are greedy.

He doesn't think you're guilty of either trait."

Avoiding the compliment, she kept her expression neutral and watched him from across the room. "Money has never been my primary goal, but I would like to be... comfortable."

"Yes," Sherman agreed, turning back to stare at her with a hooded gaze. "You do have a nice office."

"The rent is steep," she suggested quietly.

"And you're a good litigator. Your reputation is growing," he continued, ignoring her comment as if she hadn't spoken. "My client likes someone who's quick on their feet."

"I enjoy being in court."

"Pitting your wits against another's." Sherman nodded and moved back to his chair and the briefcase he'd set beside it. "If you're interested in meeting my client, give me a call. We could set something up, but it would have to be soon."

Understanding the offer was being time limited, she stood, too. "I'll check my calendar and let you know."

He stepped forward to take her hand in a firm grasp. "You're a smart woman, Christine. I know you won't let opportunity pass you by."

He let her go, and she repressed the urge to wipe her palm on her skirt. His touch left her feeling the need to rid herself of invisible dirt. "Thank you for stopping."

"My pleasure," he agreed and turned toward the door, but he stopped before opening it. "I hope you do call, Christine. I have a lot of friends, and we could do some good work together."

Her smile froze on her lips when his gaze locked once more with hers, and the air conditioning took on a decidedly personal chill. His invitation wasn't just for his client. It was from him to her. He was a widower. She was single. He wanted them to be a team. Suppressing a shudder, she nodded. "I'll get back to you."

"You do that."

The door closed behind him, her knees gave out, and she collapsed into her chair. She couldn't believe it! He'd propositioned her—in her own office! He'd asked her to become part of an operation that used every legal means available to keep criminals on the street!

Cold fury stiffened her jaw with determination. And he'd had the audacity to suggest the two of them could develop a relationship beyond seeing to the needs of any clientele.

Hissing her discontent, she shoved to her feet once more. Sherman was the worst of his kind. A bad attorney making good by helping others avoid the intent of the law. She glanced at the watch on her wrist.

Enough time had elapsed. Sherman was off the floor and on his way out of the building. That meant she could leave her office and go find David.

Marching across the suite, she pushed open his door. “David,” she began but stopped because the man by the desk wasn’t David. He was tall and blond, lean and well-muscled, and his eyes were such a pale shade of blue that they almost appeared white. Surprise collided with fear, and her fingers curled into fists. “Where’s David?”

“Here.”

The response came from her right, from the man she was looking for, and the relief that surged through her on seeing him safe and well was strong enough to make her knees knock. “I thought...”

“I’d missed your meeting?” he asked with a smile that warmed her all the way down to her toes. “Not a chance,” he denied and came forward to take her arm. “I’d like you to meet someone. This is Griffin.”

The tall blond smiled, an action that put deep slashes in his cheeks and seemed to deepen the blue of his gaze. He extended a broad hand. “Griff to my friends.”

Her fingers were lost in his. “I’ve heard about you.”

“Nothing good, I trust,” he responded tritely, obviously confident it would be otherwise.

She glanced at David. “Actually, I heard you like beer.” And tilting her head as she looked up at him. “And you do have a black eye.”

Griff blanched before cocking an eyebrow at David. “Next time, tell me to duck.”

“I did,” David grinned. “You just didn’t do it fast enough.”

Watching the exchange, sensing a depth of understanding between the two men that surpassed mere friendship, she slipped her hand into David’s. “You heard everything?”

“And nothing,” he agreed.

“I got in too late to listen in on the whole conversation, but Mr. Sherman is very careful with his words,” Griff confirmed, the thin line of his mouth testifying to his displeasure of Sherman’s ability to dance around a subject.

“I noticed,” she sighed. “But?”

David shook his head. “We still have nothing.”

“Maybe not,” Griff objected before she could. “I think I may know who his primary client is."

Christine's jaw dropped. "You do?"

"Maybe," he emphasized and looked to David. "All those court cases we looked through, I've had people trying to match up Sherman's clients with any known possible links, and we came up with a possible hit. His name's Farentino. He's a local who's trying to make it big on the criminal side of L.A., and he actually makes enough off of drugs and prostitution to get into a little money laundering."

"The briefcase," David said, and Griff nodded.

"It would fit the profile. And the connection to Sherman would make sense," Griff suggested. "Farentino would need someone like Sherman to keep his worker bees out of the slammer."

"Honor among thieves," Chris sighed.

"At least to the extent that loyalty gets rewarded," Griff agreed. "The boss hires a lawyer to keep his thugs out of jail, but only because it keeps business running."

"They pay someone to take the risks while they stay clean." Chris frowned disapproval. "But where does all that leave us?"

"With the same problem," David growled, dragging a hand through his hair. "We don't know who has the judge's son."

Griff crossed his arms over his chest and scowled blackly. "Farentino isn't known for his involvement with anything as heavy as kidnapping or armed robbery."

"Does Sherman have any other clients who might be?" Chris asked.

David shook his head. "Not that we can track down."

Disappointed, troubled and desperate, she chewed at her lip and moved forward to rest a hip against his desk. "If Farentino has never been linked with a kidnapping, it wouldn't necessarily mean he wouldn't help Sherman commit one, would it?"

David and Griff stared at her.

"You said it yourself, David," she prompted. "Someone may be looking at the possibility of getting a judge in his pocket."

David looked at Griff. "That could work for Farentino."

Griff shrugged. "It couldn't hurt him to have some pull in court. His operation's getting bigger—big enough that the L.A.PD is starting to sniff around."

"Then as Sherman's biggest client and the one with the most to gain, it stands to reason he might take a chance to help Sherman kidnap the judge's son," Chris insisted.

"Maybe," Griff agreed. "But we've already confirmed with every source we have on the street that Farentino doesn't have Wilson's kid."

"He wouldn't," she agreed. "If he's only helping."

David suddenly grinned. "She's right. He might take a chance but not commit himself to anything beyond the abduction. He wouldn't keep Jimmy Wilson himself. He wouldn't want the risk."

Griff lifted a hand to run it over his jaw. "Which means he isn't the one holding the boy. Somebody else is."

"Sherman," all three said in unison.

"No one would suspect him," Chris agreed eagerly.

"But how could he do it alone?" Griff countered. "He can't be out walking the streets and keeping an eye on the kid at the same time."

"No, he can't," she nodded in disappointment.

"But Farentino might be willing to lend a hand or a thug or two to act as guards," David quickly objected. "Remember, he has a lot to gain if Sherman succeeds with the blackmail—a judge who's willing to work for his side."

Griff's grin was sudden and bright. "Damn, all this time I've been trying to get you to sign on as part of my team. Now I might have to hire her, too. We work good together."

"Too late," David denied, grinning at and reaching out to give her a hug. "She's already my partner."

Pride at his admiration made her light headed, and she enjoyed the thrill of victory in his gaze. They still had a chance to crack the case before the Wednesday hearing date.

"We better go, buddy, if we're going to find out what assets Sherman has," Griff said, reaching out to slap David on the shoulder.

"You bet," he agreed, but he had something to do first. Without warning, he grabbed Christine and kissed her until she couldn't breathe. "Thanks, counselor."

Barely able to stand much less speak, she murmured acceptance of his flattery and watched him stride away, but when he got to the door, Griff wasn't with him.

"What are you waiting for?" David demanded and turned to find his friend, but Christine already knew where Griff was. He was staring at her with a sloppy leer on his face, and she knew without asking that he was thinking about kissing her, too.

She glanced from him to David and trembled when a gleam of warning suddenly darkened David's gaze.

"Don't even think about it, pal."

Undaunted, Griff winked at Christine. "He never did like to share."

She laughed with understanding. Griff didn't really want to hit on her. He just wanted to get David's goat. And he'd succeeded. Something she appreciated as much as he did. David was jealous.

Smiling, as both men hurried out of the office, the realization couldn't have made her happier.

THE KNOCK ON her door came late, but it wasn't unexpected. David and Griffin had left the office at about nine-thirty in the morning. Neither had ever returned, and by the time she'd left herself at six at night, no one had called either—despite her constant questioning of Mandy and Candy.

Christine didn't doubt that her behavior had erased all doubt for the twins when it came to her feelings for David, but she didn't care. She wasn't ashamed of how she felt. Besides, her concern was more for the case and for the relentless passing of precious minutes than any speculation about her personal life.

The clock was winding down. They were running out of time. It was Monday night. The hearing was Wednesday. At nine o'clock in the morning.

Hurrying to the door, she opened it without looking through the security porthole first. She knew who was waiting on the other side. She just hoped his arrival meant good news, but one look at David's face told her that he didn't have any.

Standing in the hallway, leaning against the door jam, his expression was grim, and the lines in his face said he was exhausted from the effort of trying.

Swallowing her own anxiety and the words she wanted to say, she drew him inside and, after making him sit down at the dining room table, quickly went to the kitchen to use the microwave to get him something warm to eat. He wouldn't have taken any time for food or for himself. His mission and his time had been spent for and on behalf of Judge Wilson.

Returning to the dining room minutes later with a steaming potato and leftover beef from dinner, she set it before him and let him chow down in silence. Yet she ached to ask questions, to find answers and unearth hope.

Still she remained quiet until, shoving his plate aside with a sigh, he put his elbows on the table to look across it to her. "Thanks."

"You're welcome." She reached out to touch his arm, unable to hold back any longer. "You weren't able to find anything?"

He snorted. "Sherman doesn't have much in the way of assets. A car, a house and some stocks. None of which he should have based on the price category of each. Did you know he lives in Brentwood? On the edge maybe and it's not a large estate, but what he pays in taxes, I don't earn in a year!"

Appreciating both his disgust and his frustration, she curled her fingers around his. "No other business interests?"

"None that we can locate." He shook his head. "And we searched."

She closed her eyes briefly. That meant they'd tried dummy corporations, paper trails that would lead from the legitimate to the illegitimate, and had found nothing. "What about his son's?"

"We were inside his condo looking around."

She knew better than to ask how.

"And we traced his assets, too. The condo's it, and his drug contacts are a mystery. Nobody we can pin down. Not on such short notice."

"But would they help his father help him?"

"Who knows?" David shrugged helplessly and then shook his head. "I doubt it. You're talking about a rich kid who's always been a trouble maker and who mixes with the wrong crowd. Pushing dope probably gives him a cheap thrill and a source of income besides his father's pocket. He's only nineteen."

She nodded understanding, but defeat came hard. "We knew it wouldn't be easy."

"But I was sure we could win!" His exclamation was bitter, and it took him from her as he lurched to his feet. "The only place we didn't check was his office. Maybe he's got the kid stashed in a closet."

Frowning, an idea forming, she slowly rose to join him. "Did you check his house?"

"We had it watched all day," David answered. "No one came in or out of it except for him."

"But if Jimmy Wilson is already inside—along with whoever Sherman might have watching him—you wouldn't have seen anyone coming or going."

David swung to face her, his expression clouding.

"It fits," she insisted at his doubtful frown. "Farentino won't hide a kidnap victim. It's too dangerous for him, and Sherman doesn't have anyone else he can rely on. He has nowhere else to go to. His house would be his only choice."

David's eyebrows drew together. "That's not all you're thinking."

"No," she agreed, not minding at all that he could read her so easily. "What I'm thinking is that Sherman wants me to have another meeting. Soon. Why not at his house?"

David opened his mouth to object.

"I know. I'd be on my own, but I could also get you inside," she hurriedly continued. "If he has an alarm around his estate..."

"He does."

"He'll have to shut it off to let me in."

David reached out to clutch her by the shoulders when she came around the table to stand before him. "I don't like using you as bait."

"As long as you're there to get me off the hook, I won't mind," she smiled, but her heart was pounding. With fear. For herself. For him. If they got caught, she didn't want to even think about the consequences.

"We'll need back up."

"Griffin?" she suggested.

"Someone with more power," he denied.

"Who?" she asked, but he just grinned.

Chapter 12

"WHO?" CHRISTINE prompted again when David didn't answer.

"The L.A.P,D."

She gasped. "The police?"

His gaze narrowed on her. "Got a problem with cops?"

"No, I just...I thought...won't they want to take over?"

"Sure they will, but I'm not going to let them."

"How?"

"We trade."

She blinked. "I don't understand."

"Griff says Farentino's already under investigation. That means the Department would love to find a way to nail him, and we can give it to them. Kidnapping."

"And blackmail," she breathed, but doubt lingered. "But to get Farentino, they'll have to go along with us?"

"Our plan, our way, but they get the credit." David nodded decisively. "I know just who to call. One of the guys I used to ride with just made detective. He'd love to break a case this big." He grabbed her hand to pull her toward the living room. "But before we call him, you need to call Sherman."

Pushed down into a seat next to the phone, she looked up at him. "Now?"

"He said soon, and tomorrow's Tuesday."

Swallowing trepidations and wondering at her own ability to carry the plan through, she found the phone book, looked up the number and dialed. Sherman answered on the first ring, and she wound her fingers into the receiver's cord to keep the anxiety out of her voice on hearing it. "Mark?"

"Yes?" came the quick reply.

"It's Christine Dunn," she answered, avoiding looking at David in an attempt to keep her mind on the conversation. She wanted it to be short and sweet. "I'd like to meet again. How about tomorrow night? Your house."

His hesitation was brief. His laugh loud. And appreciative. "Checked me out, huh?"

"As you did me, I'm sure," she returned primly. "Besides, I thought your client would be comfortable there."

"Yes, he would be, Chris, and he'll be very pleased with your interest," Sherman assured her with supreme confidence. "How's eight o'clock sound?"

"I'll be there." She hung up quickly and snatched her hand back from the instrument. "Eight o'clock."

David sank to his knees in front of her to cover her fingers, that were suddenly cold and trembling, with his. "I won't let anything happen to you."

Her smile was shaky. "You better not."

He reached up to cup her cheek in his hand, and she nuzzled into its solid strength. What they were about to attempt was risky. For them. For the judge. For the judge's son.

Yet reassured by his touch and knowing they were pressed for time, she glanced at the clock on the wall. "It's late. You better call Griff and let him know what's happening. You two will have to make plans. And you need to get hold of your detective friend, too."

"Later," David told her. "I've got something else I want to do first."

"What?"

"This," he said and leaned forward to capture her lips with his.

The embrace was unexpected but not unwelcome. It also titillated, teased and offered more. Yet she worried. About what they were about to do. "You're sure you shouldn't call Griff now?"

"He's a night owl. He'll be up for hours yet." He nipped her mouth with his teeth. "So will we."

Her pulse skipping with anticipation, she slipped forward on the chair to circle his neck with her arms and to rest her forehead against his. "Are you ready to show me your briefs?"

"Counselor, I'm prepared to turn over all of my evidence."

She kissed his smile. "And I get to conduct a cross-examination?"

"I'm looking forward to it." He pulled her to her knees in front of him.

"Aren't we going to the bedroom?"

"I can't wait that long," he told her. Yet despite his protest of urgency, he didn't hurry. Neither did she. Not when he took her into his arms.

There was no need to rush, no desire to speed through the moment. Instead they lingered, kneeling together, gently touching, carefully savoring the taste of each other and the quiet ignition of a need that gradually heated them both to the core.

The warmth of the flames of passion made clothing unnecessary, and hers and his were quickly shed so that they could come together again.

Touching, caressing, exploring, their limbs tangled together in a way that had their hearts beating double time and him reaching for her in selfless desperation.

He melted into her with a tenderness that brought tears to her eyes. He might not say the words. He might not be able or willing to tell her how he felt, but he loved her. At least a little, and if he wouldn't give her promises, she didn't really need any. The only thing she needed was him, and wrapping her arms around him, determined to hang onto him as long as she could, she plunged with him into the shuddering wonder of climax.

"IT'S OKAY to be scared."

Christine stood beside David on the deserted street, trunk open, ready for him to slide inside, and nodded. "Try terrified."

He kissed her quickly. Fiercely. "Just remember. You're not alone."

"We're not," she corrected, but he didn't bother to confirm it or to look around for the people he wouldn't see. He simply accepted they were there. Waiting. Watching. Willing to help if need be.

He tapped her on the nose with a finger. "Don't forget to get rid of the 'bug' as soon as you can. They might search you."

"I won't," she agreed, but her gaze was uncertain. Yet he knew she could do it. He'd taught her how to palm the electronic device that, no bigger than her thumb nail, would stick anywhere.

But the time for reassurance and talking was over. He grabbed hold of the trunk and lifted one leg into the hold. "Company's waiting, counselor."

Slipping the rest of the way inside, he pulled the lid down. The last thing he saw as he disappeared behind cold metal was her worried expression. He smothered a sigh. Obviously she still wasn't convinced he wouldn't suffocate during the ride to Sherman's house, but breathing while hidden away within the back end of her car was the least of his problems.

He was more concerned about the number of things that could go wrong. There were too many, and he went over each and every one of them as she returned to the driver's seat and started once more down the well-lit and manicured streets bordering the more exclusive residences of Brentwood.

Yet if he was prepared for the worst, he could wind up with the best. Everything could go right, too. Just as planned. Still he wouldn't take odds on it. Nobody would. Murphy's Law was a truism that seldom failed.

If something could go wrong, it would.

The most he could hope for was that it wouldn't all go wrong at once.

The car abruptly bounced, and he gritted his teeth, silently cursing the uneven cement and the car manufacturers who didn't put padding over the metal frames inside automobile's trunks. Still the gyrating and jostling didn't last long. In minutes the vehicle began to decelerate before going into a slow left turn and up a slight incline. Without being able to see, he knew they'd reached the estate's driveway.

The car stopped, and mumbled words echoed to him through the metal and fabric separating he and Christine. To get to the house, she would first have to announce herself at the voice monitor set beyond the fence that surrounded the less-than-impressive grounds circling Sherman's home, but as he expected, her clearance didn't take long. Almost immediately the car began moving again, through the metal gates Sherman would have opened by remote control, and up the curved drive.

The remainder of the drive was short, and when the Honda halted again, David silently reached for and let his hand rest on the butt of his revolver. The danger to him came now. Somebody could search her car.

Sherman or Farentino might want to make sure she was alone, that the vehicle was empty, but the distant slam of a door wasn't followed by any command to turn over the keys. Instead the echo of footsteps took her away and left him undisturbed. Yet leery. And worried. For her.

He didn't like her going off on her own into a den of snakes. It bothered him that she was by herself and vulnerable, but what choice did he have? Her plan remained the best one. Without her help, getting beyond Sherman's gate undetected would have been a minor miracle.

For a man who lived on the outskirts of the rich, for someone who possessed no known valuables beyond the real estate, Sherman's house was well protected. Overly so. The overzealous security made David even more certain Sherman's residence was not only their last hope of finding the judge's son before the hearing, but their best.

Straining to hear if anyone remained outside or near the car, his objective was simple. Get into the house, see if he could find Judge Wilson's son and get out again—as quickly as possible.

He might not be able to prevent Christine from having to meet with the likes of Sherman and Farentino, but he could insure her meeting with them was short. Once his job was done, he would give her their prearranged signal to call it quits and leave.

He eased the trunk open an inch. To accomplish that, he first had to get out of the car without anyone seeing him, and with no way of knowing where she'd parked, he wasn't sure that task was going to be as simple as he'd like. Someone could be standing nearby. He could be spotted, and his mission could end before it even began.

Staring out through the crack and into the night beyond, he attempted to get his bearings. Unfortunately, his knowledge of the layout and lighting of Sherman's home was iffy at best. He and Griffin had driven by earlier in the day. They'd also poured over the architectural plans of the structure, but they didn't know what it was like at night.

Whoever built the house hadn't included the installation of flood lights or more than a basic alarm system in his designs, but Sherman could have upgraded since moving in. He'd certainly taken great pains to get the outside perimeter of his property secure. Still any alarm should be off for the evening. Sherman would have shut it down to let Christine in, and with any luck, he would leave it off until she went out again.

That left him the lights to deal with. His first obstacle, he could see their glow on the edge of the limited vision allowed from the trunk.

Peering out, from what he could tell, the car was by the porch. A long, elaborate affair, it was more like a patio and stretched from corner to corner of the building. Lights blazed sporadically along its length, but the decorative railing installed on its edge and a line of perfectly trimmed hedges stood between the glare and him. That meant shadows. A hiding place. And hearing no sound of human presence, seeing none, he slipped out of the trunk and hurriedly rolled into the darkness.

Braced for a yell, a shout, a call of alarm, none came. Only the crickets continued to sing in the night, and huddling into the shrubs, he listened to the quiet chorus while scanning the area around him.

Beyond the bumper he was taking refuge behind lay the driveway, a long stretch of grass and the fence separating the estate from the street. To his left was blackness and the corner of the house, but to his right, just beyond the hood of the car, were the stairs leading up to the front door.

Gazing through the hedge toward the entrance way, he frowned. The entire area was caught in a ring of light thrown by an overhead bulb. He was going to have to find another way inside, probably through the rear of the house.

Keeping himself as small as possible, he crept away from the car and the steps and toward the far corner of the porch, and he went slowly. His dark clothing provided good camouflage. He would blend in with the shadows, but shadows didn't move.

During the day, after he and Griff's visit, Griff's people had remained to watch Sherman's residence. No guards were spotted during the surveillance, but it paid to be cautious.

Reaching the edge of darkness veiling the long porch, David paused to listen again to the night. Except for the crickets, quiet was the only thing to be heard. No one else was patrolling the grounds with him.

Relieved, slowly straightening to his full height beside the hedge, he prepared to make a break for what cover he could find along the side of the house, but one step was all he took before somebody coughed.

David froze. He wasn't alone. Somebody was in the blackness with him.

Afraid to move, he waited. Had he been seen? His heart hammered in his chest in anticipation, but no one came out of the night to challenge him. Silence reigned until, unexpectedly, somebody cleared their throat.

David ducked. Whoever was outside was around the corner from where he was. They couldn't see him, and he couldn't see them.

Dropping to his hands and knees, he scooted to the very edge of the hedge, looked past it and almost immediately spotted a silhouette. A man was leaning against a sedan. The car was parked out of sight of the drive and on the far side of the house.

Gritting his teeth in frustration, David pulled back behind the hedge once more. Big and black the vehicle had to belong to Farentino, and the man beside it must, too. Posing as a chauffeur, the silhouette probably also doubled as a bodyguard. David frowned. But if that was true, why wasn't the man in the house with his boss?

Swearing silently David jerked back to look at one of the windows beyond the porch. The thug by the car wasn't inside with Farentino because he didn't need to be. He wasn't acting as a bodyguard. His only duty was to drive. The bodyguard duties would belong to the second henchman Farentino would have brought with him—the one inside with Christine!

David's gaze jumped to the front door of the house. It was too late to warn Christine. He couldn't tell her Sherman and Farentino weren't the only ones waiting for her. They would have someone else with them—maybe more than one someone else. Armed and dangerous hired guns, if she said the wrong thing, if she was caught with the device in her hand, she was dead, and he was too damn far away to even try to stop it!

"CHRISTINE."

Sherman's greeting was warm as she stepped into his foyer, but she didn't come through the door alone. She was escorted by one of the men who'd been waiting for her outside. The other, as far as she knew, was still at the gate.

Arriving at Sherman's home, expecting to use a voice box to request entrance to the estate, she'd found a man waiting instead. Another, the one immediately behind her, was by the porch when she parked.

Glancing from Sherman to her business-suited escort, who she strongly suspected was armed, she swallowed fear. David didn't know about the additional manpower in the house. Stuck in the trunk of her car, he had no idea the number of players in the game had changed and the level of danger with it, and she couldn't warn him. He was on his own. As was she.

Praying for his safety, she forced her lips to curve as Sherman took her one hand in both of his. The other she kept firmly on her purse—and around the tiny device resting in her palm. "Mark, I wasn't expecting your house to be so...crowded."

He laughed and led her to the right and into an elaborately decorated den. "You mean our protectors for the evening. I'm afraid I can't claim them as mine."

"Nevertheless, I'm impressed." And intimidated, but if she couldn't warn David, at least she could warn the others. Griff and David's detective friend, Rudy Berman, who were waiting outside the gate. The "bug" she was holding was for their benefit—and hers. One word and they would rush to her rescue, but she didn't want them to chance it without being aware of what they'd be up against. "A man on the gate and another inside with you. Is all of this security really necessary?"

"My friend likes to be cautious, Chris," Sherman assured her with a casual shrug. "He has to be, as I'm sure you can understand. That's why I need you to give me your purse."

Her heart leapt into her throat. Releasing her bag meant palming the tiny piece of metal, and hanging onto it until she could find some place and something to transfer it to.

"And this gentleman behind you will just need to use this metal detector," Sherman continued, gesturing to the guard who had brought her in from outside. "Just in case you're wired."

She gulped, fighting for indignance and time. "You think I went to the police?"

"Like I said," Sherman sighed. "We have to be cautious."

Glaring at the sentry standing ready to her left and presented with little choice, she nodded. "Fine." But, rather than simply hand Sherman her purse, she shoved it at him and immediately spun toward the guard. The quickness of her movements she hoped were enough to fool both sets of eyes as she dropped her hand and tossed the "bug" backwards onto the carpet.

It wasn't the ideal solution, but it was the only one open to her—and holding her breath, she waited for a metallic clink to give her away. If the listening device rolled into or hit some piece of furniture, her charade would be over, but no tell-tale sound came. No unexplained rattle followed to damn her for her actions. The room remained quiet as the search was performed.

Quick and unproductive, in less than a minute the guard gave a silent nod to Sherman before walking away, and Sherman handed back the purse he'd gone through. "That was painless now, wasn't it?"

She snatched it from his hand and fought not to look down at the floor. Could she have broken David's electronic gadget? And what if the coming meeting took her beyond the room they were in and so the ear of those beyond the gate? She lifted her chin in defiance of the tremors running through her. "Your search may have been painless, but it was also unnecessary. We're not doing anything illegal, are we?"

"Of course not," was the reply, but it didn't come from Sherman. It came from her left and from a man entering the room from a second doorway.

Small in build, he couldn't be over five seven, and with thinning hair and dark eyes hidden behind wire-rimmed glasses, he looked to be a clerk, a bookkeeper, or maybe an accountant, but he wasn't. She recognized him from the photograph Griffin had shown her earlier that day. He was Angelo Farentino, and he was the criminal mind behind a good many crimes in Los Angeles. The L.A.P.D. just needed help proving it.

"I'm glad you could come, Ms. Dunn," Farentino greeted, continuing his approach to extend and take her hand in a gentle grip.

His palm against hers was warm, but the sound of his voice sent a chill down her spine. He was the one who had made the midnight call days before. He was who had threatened her, who would have seen her killed, and it was all she could do not to yank her fingers from his. "I hope I will be, too."

He smiled and released her to gesture toward the chairs and sofas clustered around a large, stained glass coffee table set out before a fireplace. The entire ensemble cost, she was sure, more than furnishing her entire condo. "Let's sit and talk."

Moving to one of the chairs, she forced herself to relax back into the brocaded padding. What she was about to do was what she did for a living. Negotiate. Set terms. Reach an agreement. If this wasn't a usual mediation conference, she needed to try to treat it like one.

Facing the two men who took seats opposite her, both appeared very pleased with themselves. With her. She nearly choked on her own disgust but swallowed it instead. "Mark has given me the impression that you employ his services with a retainer."

Farentino nodded. "Yes, I'm responsible for paying his rent and making sure he has everything he needs to run his office. It's my way of insuring he has no distractions or obligations which might prevent him from giving both me and my employees his full attention and the best legal advice he can provide."

Shocked at the depth of the bribery, the amount, her hesitant stammer reflected honest surprise. "That's very generous."

"And very beneficial to both parties, wouldn't you agree, Mark?"

Sherman nodded. "Very."

"Your employees," she said, turning back to Farentino. "They often have legal...difficulties?"

"It's part of their occupation."

"Which is?" she pressed.

"Delivery of goods mostly," Farentino evaded, but she needed him to be more specific for the men beyond the gate.

"Such as what was in the briefcase?" she asked.

"On occasion."

"I'd be remiss as an attorney if I didn't point out to you that carrying thousands of dollars in cash is risky. It could be easily lost."

"True," Farentino conceded. "And as you know, it has happened. When it does, we make every effort to find it—as we did with the case you received."

"And the reason you have your employees carry cash?" she asked. "Surely those you work with accept a check?"

Farentino's smile was mild. "Those I deal with prefer direct payment."

"Which would lead many to believe whatever business you're conducting is illegal." She tilted her head to the side. "Just why did you have that much cash in the courthouse? Not a bribe, surely?"

"Nothing so dramatic, I assure you," Farentino dismissed with a wave of his hand. "The courthouse was simply a convenient place to make an exchange."

"One briefcase for another," she concluded. "One filled with cash and the other with..."

Farentino's smile widened. "Is it important for you to know?"

"It's important I know what your business entails if I'm going to be representing you."

"Perhaps the less you know the better."

"The better for who?" she asked. "You? Or me?"

"What do you think?" Farentino returned, his smile still in place and his eyes bright with the enjoyment of the game.

"I think," she told him, "that I wouldn't like to take on a client whose endeavors might see me spend my career behind bars."

Farentino gestured to Sherman who had taken a chair to his left. "Mark has worked for me for years and never once been questioned by the police because what he does for me is totally legal."

"And what you do for him?" she asked, thinking of the judge's son.

"I reward him for being a good employee by seeing, professionally, he lacks for nothing."

"His generosity sees I lack for nothing personally either," Sherman put in and gestured to the room around him. "A nice home for me and my son."

"Your son," she nodded and forged quickly into the unwitting opening in the conversation. "I heard he had some difficulty with the police."

Sherman shrugged. "The exuberance of youth. I'm sure we'll be able to set everything right at his hearing tomorrow."

"You're sure of your skills," she stated as if in approval, but his smile denied her reasoning.

"I'm sure the judge will see things my way."

"Which court did you get?"

"Judge Wilson's."

She lifted an eyebrow. "He's tough."

"He can be reasonable," Farentino interrupted. "Or haven't you found him to be so?"

Biting her tongue to prevent herself from accusing him of blackmail, she struggled for a way to gain a confession but couldn't find one. Not without a direct attack. "Yes, he's a good judge, although he takes a hard line on crime."

She glanced from Farentino to Sherman and back again.

"Your method of payment for services, Mr. Farentino, is certainly more than I could expect, but I am concerned about some of the things I've heard regarding Mr. Sherman's clientele and, presumably, your employees."

"A lawyer can't judge who walks through the door," Sherman objected, drawing her attention back to him. "Our job, Chris, is not to choose who we defend but to defend those who choose us."

"True," she agreed. "However, a lawyer has an obligation to insure that both he and his clients remain within the boundaries of the law."

"You will never be asked to do anything that would break the law," Farentino guaranteed with a solemn nod. "Your only task will be to interpret the law so that it is applied in the best interests of myself and the people who work for me."

"Legal loop holes?" she queried.

"Legal remedies," Farentino denied and looked to Sherman. "Mark, I could use something to drink. How about you, Christine? May I call you Christine?"

"Of course," she confirmed, noting both the surprise and the flash of resentment in Sherman's expression at the order to serve, but he didn't protest against Farentino's bidding.

Rising he plastered a smile on his face. "My oversight. I'm being a poor host. What can I offer you, Chris? Wine, perhaps?"

"Fine," Farentino answered for her and dismissed Sherman with a wave of his hand. Sherman's lips tightened, but Farentino only had eyes for her. Leaning forward as Sherman moved away, he kept his voice low and murmured, "I'm in need of someone with your talents, Christine."

"But Mark..."

"Mark is a fine attorney, but he doesn't possess your skills."

"I..." she started to protest, but Farentino shook his head.

"You've become quite a good litigator, I understand," Farentino soothed. "Trials were never Mark's specialty."

The inference was clear and put a lump in her throat. Farentino wanted to move her in and Sherman out. Sherman had outlived his usefulness and had, perhaps, pushed his importance too far by requesting Farentino's assistance in a kidnapping to protect personal interests. "I see."

"I'm not sure that you do, but I believe I can convince you."

Coming back into hearing range and carrying a small tray with three glasses, Sherman was quick to agree. "Mr. Farentino can be very persuasive."

Accepting one of the long-stemmed flutes filled with white wine, she sipped the beverage without tasting its flavor and struggled to keep her hand steady. How badly did Farentino want Sherman out of the way? Enough to commit murder?

Murmuring agreement when Farentino commented on the quality of the wine, she wished for escape. The meeting was proving to be more than she bargained for, but she couldn't—wouldn't—go without David. And she had no idea where he was.

Was he still in the trunk of the car, unable to get out because of the guard posted at the gate? Had that guard followed her up to the house? Was he watching the front door, preventing David from going anywhere? Or was David inside somewhere nearby?

Smiling as Farentino proposed a toast, she hoped he was close. Very close. But she would have been surprised if she knew how near to her he actually was.

Creeping up the staircase to the second floor, David paused to listen before stepping out onto the landing. Behind him was the first floor. After making a complete circle of the house to avoid detection by Farentino's chauffeur, he'd gained entrance through an easily compromised lock on the back door.

From there he'd scouted the lower level of Sherman's home as best he could with all the lights burning on that floor and with a guard in the hall, and he'd managed to eliminate the basement as a possible hiding place for the judge's son. Now he had to do the upstairs. In one of the bedrooms he hoped to hit pay dirt and find Jimmy Wilson.

Letting his eyes adjust to the near total darkness in the upper corridor, he could still hear the murmured conversation from below. Christine was talking. She was all right and holding her own, but he wanted to get her out of the house.

The men she was with were criminals. Maybe not convicted. They'd never been unlucky enough to get caught, but he wanted to change that and he wanted her out of their reach.

Stepping forward, he hugged the wall and cautiously headed for the first closed door. No guard appeared to be posted in the hall, but in the blackness it was impossible to be sure. Farentino had men outside and on the lower floor. Chances were good another armed thug was loitering somewhere, and his instincts proved true when, about to grab the handle, up ahead a shadow within a shadow moved.

Squinting, holding himself perfectly still, he waited to confirm what he suspected. He wasn't alone. Again. Another man was in the hall, but he wasn't anywhere near the second staircase standing between he and David. He was too far away from the steps to be able to run if Farentino called.

David's mouth thinned. This sentry wasn't someone Farentino had brought with him for the night. This guard, he suspected, had been in Sherman's home for some time—since, perhaps, Jimmy Wilson's disappearance.

Cursing Sherman and Farentino and the stranger standing in front of the door he was suddenly certain was the one he had to get into, David considered his options.

Getting to the door unseen was going to be a difficult trick to manage, but he had to try. That or go back outside, confirm to Griffin and Rudy Berman that the judge's son was inside under lock and key, and let them come get him out. The latter choice didn't appeal to him. He didn't like the idea of quitting before the job was done, especially when it would mean leaving Christine alone. And exposed.

Any unexpected police presence might panic Farentino. Not only did the man know the police were after him—he'd been hauled in for questioning more than once—he was also aware a kidnap victim was sitting in a room on the floor above him. If confronted, Farentino could decide to fight rather than chance arrest and prison, and if he and his henchmen started to shoot, she'd be trapped in the cross-fire. David wasn't going to risk that. He wasn't going to risk her. But he could risk himself.

He had a chance, a slim one, of getting through the guard and to Jimmy Wilson undetected. If he did, he could take the boy out, give Christine the all clear, and with he and the judge's son in her trunk, the three of them could roll right out of the gate to safety with Sherman and Farentino none the wiser. Until it was too late.

Taking a deep, steadying breath, David shoved off from the wall and started strolling down the hall with an arrogant amble. He was going to have to pretend. If he acted as if he belonged, the guard wouldn't react to his unexpected presence and call out. He would wait in silence until David walked right up to and hit him....

Chapter 13

"I WAS ONCE like you, Chris," Sherman said, leaning forward to set his wine flute on the intricately engraved coffee table sitting between them. "Young, idealistic, ready to charge out into the world to right all wrongs. I wanted to be the champion of lost causes, but you're finding out what I did."

Christine watched him gesture expressively.

"The real world isn't what you dream it is in law school. Clients are hard to find, and when you get one, they can't afford to pay you. And instead of spending your time arguing appeals, your days are spent in divorce court where you're caught in between two people who hate each other."

"It's hard to get started," she admitted, remembering the first few months of scraping and scrimping, but she hadn't given up. And she hadn't given in either. Not to temptation, not to the likes of Farentino. Most young lawyers didn't. They beat the books and the pavement until they made profit enough to say they were making a living, but Sherman obviously had taken a shorter route to success.

"And when you do finally get that good case, the one you've been dreaming of, the judge rules against you, or some clever and more experienced attorney comes along and convinces the jury he's right and you're wrong and you lose the case you should have won."

"What Mark means," Farentino suggested. "Is that practicing law is hard enough without having to worry about rent and office supplies and other trivialities. Your time should be devoted to taking care of your clients. If you can expend all your time and energy on your work, you can use your knowledge to advantage—and make sure you always win."

"You mean make sure the client wins," she corrected, not mentioning the cost of such devotion to duty. A total loss of ethics. Instead of interpreting a statute written to protect the innocent, it was purposefully and artfully twisted into a reason to help the guilty.

"If we win, you win," Farentino smiled kindly. "And to prove our faith in you and your ability to help us, we're willing to offer you a beginning bonus."

She watched Farentino nod at Sherman who rose without

prompting to retrieve a briefcase from behind the sofa. She recognized it immediately. It was a duplicate of her own, of the one she'd picked up by mistake days before, and it didn't take much deduction to guess what it held.

"This looks familiar to you, I'm sure," Farentino told her and stood to join Sherman as he set the attaché on the coffee table. "And I believe you know what it contains, but let me show you."

Even expecting to see the money, it was difficult not to gasp out loud at the sight of the number of bills inside. The case wasn't as full as it had been before. The amount of money within it was easily halved, but the total still had to be in the thousands.

Trying to think of something to say, trying to figure out how she could turn the offer down without putting herself—or the evening mission—in jeopardy, she stammered and abruptly jumped when a thud echoed through the house.

Loud, the noise came from upstairs, and her first thought was for David. She jumped to her feet in alarm. "What was that?"

Sherman, staring at the ceiling, shook his head with a frown. "I don't know."

Beside him, Farentino immediately jerked a thumb at the guard who appeared in one of the room's doorways. The man nodded, drew a revolver, and rushed out of sight and up some stairs Christine couldn't see.

Her first instinct was to scream a warning. Yet it wasn't necessary. If she could hear the charge, if it was David on the upper floor, he would hear it, too. And he would protect himself. Just as she needed to protect herself.

Swinging on Sherman, prepared to use the distraction to escape from the house and to rendezvous with David outside, she grabbed her purse and stepped backwards toward the front door. "Maybe I'm the one who should have searched for wires," she snapped. "Maybe this is a set up, and you're looking for someone to give to the police."

"Christine..." he began.

"I'm leaving." Yet before she could take another step, a second crash sounded. It was followed by several more as someone fell down the steps in the hall and landed at the bottom with a bang. Her hesitation gave Farentino the chance to grab her arm.

"You're not going anywhere," he denied and jammed a small gun into her rib cage. "The proposition you've been offered is irrevocable. You either say yes now and leave as our partner, or you say no and die."

AT THE TOP of the stairs, David heard the threat and swore under his breath. He'd managed to eliminate both guards, but he'd made more noise in the process than the proverbial elephant in a china shop.

Cursing his own ineptitude, he hurried to the bedroom door, stepped over the other fallen guard, and burst inside. Only one person was within. A young man. Sitting in a chair, he was gagged, tied and staring at him in terror.

David strode to his side and started yanking on the knots holding Jimmy Wilson in place. "My name's Maverick, and you're getting out of here."

It took less than a minute to get him beyond the room and into the hall, and with no more guards appearing to defend or attack, David knew it was a safe bet Farentino's entourage for the evening numbered three. That meant it was safe to send the judge's son out on his own.

Offering quick instructions, he pointed the way to the far staircase and the back door. Once out of the house and on the grounds, Jimmy could hide until Griffin and Rudy came through the front gate—something David figured they were already doing.

Watching Jimmy disappear from sight, David swung back to the second staircase leading to the lower floor—the one he'd just shoved one of Farentino's thugs down—and listened. He might have gotten Jimmy Wilson out of danger, but Christine was still trapped and the sound of angry voices said she was in trouble.

With a shout, he got their attention away from her.

"Sherman!"

His call brought silence and, for Christine, relief. David was safe!

"I've got the judge's son, Sherman!" David's voice came again. "And I'm taking him with me!"

Caught in Farentino's grip, Christine was dragged along when Farentino whirled to hiss at Sherman. "You fool! Someone's found you out!"

"That's impossible!" Sherman flared hotly, but Christine was willing to take advantage of his confusion.

"Judge's son?" she demanded, ignoring the hard metal muzzle pressed into her side. "You kidnapped a judge's son?"

"I didn't," Sherman growled and pointed to Farentino. "His men did to help me save *my* son."

Nearly grinning at the confession, praying Griffin was still listening, still recording, she gasped when Sherman jumped around the couch, yanked open a cabinet drawer and pulled out a black revolver.

As she watched, he ran with it to the doorway.

"You try to leave this house, you're dead and so's the boy!"

Farentino jerked Christine toward the doorway, too. "And you'll be responsible for the death of an innocent victim. A young woman who I'm presently holding a gun on."

Christine cried out when her arm was given a sudden and vicious twist.

"Why don't you come on down, and we'll talk about this," Farentino reasoned, barely easing his hold on her. "Or should I call my men in from outside and start shooting now?"

With her shoulder on fire, with searing agony blurring her vision, she stared into the hallway beyond the room and used her teeth to clamp down hard on her lip. She wouldn't make another sound. She wouldn't, but the effort cost her. In her mouth she tasted blood. Hers. But better hers than David's. Yet even as she strove to remain silent and prayed for him to go, to get out with Jimmy Wilson, David stepped into view.

Dressed all in black, his gun still in his hand as his arms hung limp at his sides, his gaze held pure hatred for the man who held her by his side.

"David."

Her word was a whisper, but Farentino heard it.

"So you know one another." He looked to Sherman who was holding his revolver on David. "It was a trap."

"And you're the one who's about to be caught in it," David confirmed. "The police are outside, and when they get in here, you're going to have a lot of questions to answer, especially about Jimmy Wilson."

Farentino laughed. "You're bluffing. If you're working with the police, why are you in here? Alone?"

David shrugged, eying Farentino who had Christine plastered to his side, but at least his weapon wasn't on her. The small silver automatic was in Farentino's grip, but he wasn't prepared to use it. He was waving it around as he spoke. His finger wasn't even on the trigger. Feeling the cold and heavy weight of his Glock in his palm, David wasn't at such a disadvantage. He was prepared to fire. He could take Farentino out with one shot. He was quick enough, he was good enough, but he wouldn't be able to get Sherman, too.

"That's right, David, is it?" Sherman asked. "Your bumbling attempt to release the boy has saved us from making a big mistake."

"And I'll pay for it," David agreed, certain Griffin and the police would barge in any minute—and get Christine killed. He smiled at her. "I'm sorry, babe."

She screamed as he raised his gun, and the front door crashed open.

Bullets whined, Farentino jerked, and she pulled free to dive for the floor. But the shooting continued.

It boomed around her. Slamming her hands over her ears, she tried to block out the deadly racket, but huddled in a ball, she wasn't thinking of herself. She was thinking of David.

Was he all right? Had he been shot?

Straining to see around the massive collage of sofas, chairs and coffee table, she'd fallen behind, she couldn't find him. Where was he?

Fearing the worst, terror clogging her throat, she began to crawl to where he'd been standing. The whistle of lead didn't stop her. Neither did the shouted commands echoing around the room. On her hands and knees, she kept going, past Farentino who lay groaning behind her and toward the hall. "David!"

He didn't answer.

"David!"

Her second shout unexpectedly fell into deafening silence. The battle was over. The last bullet had been fired, and the lingering cry of it mixed with the acrid smell of gun powder as dread scorched her heart.

A sob locked in her throat. "David!"

"Chris!"

"David!" Scrambling faster, she cleared a chair and nearly collided with Sherman. He was sprawled across the carpet and bleeding, but she barely spared him a glance. "David!"

He didn't respond again, but he didn't have to. Rounding another chair, she spotted him stretched out on the floor.

Panic carried her to his side. "Are you all right?"

He caught her arm. "Are you?"

She didn't answer as she helped him sit up. She didn't care about herself. It was him she was worried about, but searching for wounds, she saw none. He wasn't injured. He hadn't been shot. Relief collided with lingering terror, and she slammed her fist into his chest. "You idiot! You could have been killed!"

He yelped and dodged her second blow.

"Why didn't you stay up stairs?"

He caught her wrist when she swung again. "Because I was worried about you."

"Oh." Mollified but not sure she should forgive him, she tried to blink the tears from her eyes and brush the agony from her heart, but it was hard. Nearly impossible. She huffed indignantly to hide the effort and her pain. She'd almost lost him. He'd almost died because of her. "I can take care of myself," she reminded him with a sniff.

"That's gratitude for you."

Trapped by his grin, she put out a trembling hand to touch his face and despite her best efforts, a tear slipped free. "Are you really all right?"

"As long as you are," he admitted, his fingers catching hers. "Because I don't think I could go on living if you weren't."

Lost in the warmth of his gaze, words deserted her.

"I love you, counselor."

More tears spilled over. "Oh, David."

He caught her when she threw herself against him.

"You silly man." But she liked the feel of his arms around her. She liked that he *was* a man. "I love you, too."

He held her close. "I suppose this means we should get married."

"Are you asking?" she demanded, pulling back to glare at him. "Or telling?"

"Begging."

He swallowed her laugh with a kiss, but a throat clearing above them broke the embrace. Glancing up with David, she found Griffin standing over them.

"I hate to break this reunion up," Griff apologized. "But I need to know where the kid is."

"Outside," David answered. "I told him to find a bush and hide until the cavalry arrived."

Griffin nodded and started to walk away.

"By the way, what the hell took you so long?" David demanded.

"The guard at the gate was reluctant to let us in," Griff grunted in disgust. "I had to go over the fence."

And if he hadn't, if he hadn't climbed the fence, if he hadn't broken the front door in exactly when he had, with two guns on him, David would have died. Rising to her feet, Christine stepped forward to press a grateful kiss to Griffin's cheek. "Thank you."

His pale eyes brightened as he looked from her to David. "No thanks necessary. Just take care of him."

"You have my word on that," she promised and slipped back to David who had followed her up to stand, too.

He gave her shoulders a squeeze as Griffin disappeared into the shadows at the end of the hall and turned with her to face the den.

Uniformed police officers were collecting Sherman and Farentino from the floor. Both men were bleeding but moving on their own. They'd live to have their day in court. A tremor shuddered through her. Justice had prevailed. The good guys had won, and looking past the men to the briefcase filled with cash, she watched the police gather it, too—as evidence.

She sighed. "I suppose I'll have to give that pack of money back."

"I suppose," David agreed, his hip resting comfortably against hers as they continued to stand together. "Disappointed?"

She let her head drop back against his shoulder as she looked up at him. "I got what I wanted."

His smile blended with hers in a quick embrace. "Me, too."

Content, happy the crisis was over, she lifted a hopeful eyebrow. "Can we go home now?"

"Your place or mine?" he asked, turning from the chaos around them to steer her toward the front door.

"Mine," she sighed. "I have to feed Arthur."

David nodded. "Do you think he can get used to having a man in his life?"

"I think he already has. Just like me."

Stopping on the front porch, he brought her into his arms once more, and it was some time before he led her down the steps to her car.

Epilogue

"SO WHAT DO you think?"

The demand came from Griffin, and puzzled but intrigued by the summons that had brought both she and David to some vacant offices on the tenth floor of their building, Christine sighed at all the space and windows around her. "It's big and airy, and I envy you if you're going to be moving in here to work."

"Don't envy me," Griffin responded. "Join me."

"Join..."

"Griff wants us to move in here with him," David told her. "His office is too small for expansion. He needs some place bigger, but he also wants some help."

"I want partners," Griff clarified, shoving his hands in his pockets to prowl through the empty rooms. "I'd like them to be you."

"Be flattered," David told her when she found it impossible to speak. "Griff wouldn't invite just any attorney to share space with him."

"You're okay, counselor," Griff confirmed gruffly, turning from his pacing to join her where she stood in the center of the suite. "Even if you nearly broke my ear drum."

She smothered a laugh. When tossing the electronic listening device to the floor on entering Sherman's house a week before, she hadn't thought about the effects on anyone listening. Her only concern had been getting rid of it. "I'm sorry."

Griff shrugged. "At least you threw it on a carpet."

And the landing, fortunately, *hadn't* hurt the piece of metal one bit—even if the collision with the floor had caused shock waves in Griffin's head. The tiny beacon had kept working and picked up every word spoken with a crystal clarity that had their friend and detective Rudy Berman laughing all the way to court. Mark Sherman was singing—loud and long and to anyone willing to listen.

On arrest Sherman had, at first, steadfastly refused to cooperate, but his tune had changed dramatically when Rudy played the tape of his admission to being involved in a kidnapping.

Outraged, compromised, realizing he was in hot water, Sherman had suddenly rethought his position and entered into a plea bargain agreement. The charges against him would be limited to kidnapping. They would not include blackmail, attempted murder, conspiracy, racketeering and drug running. In exchange for the reduction, he was helping the police go through his records to find every piece of paper he had to help condemn Farentino.

Sherman would still be going to jail for a long time, probably for life without parole with the extenuating circumstances, but he wasn't going alone. He was taking Farentino with him by his willingness to turn state's evidence, and Rudy Berman couldn't be happier.

Just promoted to detective a few months earlier, he was being credited with cracking a major case, and under his guidance, the L.A.P.D. was disassembling Farentino's drug operation. Several arrests had already been made and more would follow, but the illegal sale and distribution of drugs wasn't the only activity that would see Farentino put behind bars. He was also facing kidnapping and blackmail charges along with the attempted murder of she and David.

"I'll remember next time," she told Griffin sympathetically.

"She's only a beginner after all," David offered on her behalf, entwining his fingers with hers.

"Yeah, well, you did good," Griff acknowledged grudgingly. "Even if you are an attorney."

David grinned, and she did, too. David had filled her in on Griffin's abhorrence of lawyers and judges.

"Thank you, Griff."

"Don't thank me. Just think about this," he said, pulling one hand from his pocket to gesture to the space and walls around them. "This could be ours instead of mine." He looked past her to David. "I have to let the landlord know by the end of the week."

"We'll get back to you today."

With a nod to Christine, Griffin left, and when he was out the door and she was alone with David, she lifted her face to his. "You knew about this?"

"He mentioned it while we were working on the case," David admitted.

"And you're interested."

"Not enough to leave you."

Warmth born of love and trust flooded through her, and she squeezed the fingers holding hers before slowly moving away to walk through the massive suite. Altogether the rooms covered at least a third of the floor—instead of a tiny block such as she and David currently rented.

Stopping in a corner office to admire the towering glass and steel buildings of Los Angeles from two angles at the same time, her teeth worried her lower lip.

Throughout her years at law school, never had she imagined being part of a big operation. Her goal, always, was to be independent. She wanted to be able to call her own shots, make her own decisions, but the last week had changed her thinking. Just as it had changed her life.

Moving closer to one of the windows, she stared down at the traffic below. It was Wednesday morning and just after eight o'clock. Rush hour was in full swing, and the sun was climbing up from the eastern horizon.

"Quite a view," David said, joining her.

"It is a few floors up from what we're used to." she admitted and turned to look at him. He was trying to hide it, but he was anxious about her decision. "You want to do this."

He moved his shoulders in a noncommittal motion. "I want to do what Griff is doing, and I will whether I work with him or not. It would be easier by joining someone who already has his foot in the door, but I've started from scratch before. And he'd still help me whether we were partners or not."

She nodded. He was talking about bounty hunting. Finding people who skipped their court hearings rather than appear and answer for whatever they'd done. It was an occupation Hollywood liked to glamorize. The movies and television made the job seem exotic. It wasn't. It was dangerous. Or it could be if proper precautions weren't taken.

About eighty percent of all arrests made by bail enforcement agents were quiet and uneventful. She'd learned that from a friend after realizing David was interested in that end of the private investigation business, but she wasn't really worried. She trusted him not to take unnecessary risks while doing his job—and when it came to her.

"Do you think the twins would mind?" she asked, putting her back to the pane of glass and the view of the city to gaze up at him.

"I hope not," David told her. "I think Griff wants them more than he does us."

She frowned. "He doesn't have a secretary?"

"One, and she's everything the twins aren't. Loud, demanding and ferocious."

"You've met her?" Christine asked.

David nodded. "She scares the hell out of me, but that's probably how she keeps the other investigators in line."

"How many are there?"

"Five."

"You'd make six," she observed.

"Griff says he'll stop at an even dozen."

She nodded understanding. "He knows what he wants."

David smiled. "So do I."

The heat in his gaze made her pulse jump, but he wasn't trying to use her feelings for him to influence or sway. The decision to join with Griffin was her own, but it wasn't difficult to make up her mind.

Helping the judge was already having ramifications. Her name was now known by the police, and David wasn't the only one who was receiving their referrals. She, like Judge Wilson, was considered a friend, someone to be counted on to see the law was enforced with the mind set with which it was written, and she liked the feeling their appreciation gave her.

"I think this would be a good move for us," she announced and paced away to stand in the middle of the big room. "Do you think Griffin would let me have this office?"

David grinned, realizing it was the biggest one in the suite. "We could make it a condition."

She grinned, too. "We could, couldn't we?"

"Absolutely," he agreed, moving forward to settle his hands on her hips as they faced each other. His smile vanished. "You're sure?" he questioned. "You're not doing this because of me?"

"No," she denied, circling his waist with her arms. "I'm doing it because of us. We're going to need help, too. You with your bounty hunting and me with all the new cases I'm going to be handling because of the contacts Griff is going to bring us."

Obviously relieved and grateful for her agreement, he pressed his lips to her forehead. "You realize we're going to need your help as much as your clients will. We'll have to have an attorney to keep us out of trouble."

"Griff seems to think I can handle it."

"I know you can."

She smiled and offered her lips to him, satisfied with herself, eager for the challenges of the future and in love with the man she was going to share them with. "We're going to be late," she told him when he lifted his head from hers.

"Ah," he acknowledged. "The hearing for Sherman's son."

"I think Judge Wilson would like us to be there."

"I'm sure he would," David agreed, steering her toward the door and the elevator beyond. "We can watch with him from the cheap seats."

She laughed and stepped into the car with him to make the ride to their office floor. "I'm glad he voluntarily recused himself and is letting another judge handle the sentencing."

"That's why the hearing got delayed a week and why he's so well respected. He wasn't going to give Sherman's son a cause to appeal." David shrugged as the doors closed with an audible mechanical swish. "He wants to make sure the son joins the father where they both belong. In jail."

"I'm not going to give you a chance to appeal either, you know."

Surprised but willing, he grinned as she cornered him in the elevator. "Mandatory sentence?" he asked, pinned to the wall by the woman who'd proven him wrong. Not everyone was afraid of risk. Not everyone was intimidated by a patch. Especially her.

"Life for sure," she confirmed and lifted her face to his.

"I hope there won't be an opportunity for parole," he murmured, brushing his mouth across hers.

She shuddered and melted against him, belying the cool crispness of her appearance. Her prim suit and swept up hair couldn't hide the heat that burned within her for him, and he enjoyed the flames. "Not a chance," she denied. "Once the sentence is given, I'm going to lock you up and throw away the key."

"Take me away," he ordered, and bent his head again.

Neither one of them moved when the bell rang and the elevator doors opened. They were both already where they wanted to be.

~ * ~

Kimberly Grey

Kim's writing career began with a school assignment. When her 9th grade teacher requested everyone write a short story, she ended up penning her first tale of romantic suspense!

From that initial teenage motorcycle melodrama, Kim went on to publish books with both Leisure and Harlequin before entering the world of "e" where her books have all been well received by reviewers and readers.

When not writing, Kim enjoys gardening and reading and playing with her two cats, Squirt and Small Fry, who serve as inspiration for the friendly felines who sometimes appear in her stories. Write to her by email at kimgrey@yahoo.com or check out her web page at http://www.kimberlygrey.com.

Printed in the United States
26169LVS00001B/10-21